The
Lieutenant

ALSO BY KATE GRENVILLE

NOVELS
Lilian's Story
Dark Places
Dreamhouse
Joan Makes History
The Idea of Perfection
The Secret River

SHORT STORIES
Bearded Ladies

NON-FICTION
The Writing Book
Making Stories (with Sue Woolfe)
Writing from Start to Finish
Searching for the Secret River

The
Lieutenant

KATE
GRENVILLE

Atlantic Monthly Press
New York

SEP 0 8 2009[1]

First published in Australia in 2008 by The Text Publishing Company

Printed in the United States of America

FIRST AMERICAN EDITION

ISBN-13: 978-0-8021-1916-2

Atlantic Monthly Press
an imprint of Grove/Atlantic, Inc.
841 Broadway
New York, NY 10003
Distributed by Publishers Group West
www.groveatlantic.com

09 10 11 12   10 9 8 7 6 5 4 3 2 1

*Dedicated to Patyegarang and the Cadigal people
and William Dawes.
Their story inspired this work of fiction.*

CONTENTS

PART ONE

The Young Lieutenant

✳

Daniel Rooke was quiet, moody, a man of few words. He had no memories other than of being an outsider.

At the dame school in Portsmouth they thought him stupid. His first day there was by coincidence his fifth birthday, the third of March 1767. He took his place behind the desk with his mother's breakfast oatmeal cosy in his stomach and his new jacket on, happy to be joining the world beyond his home.

Mrs Bartholomew showed him a badly executed engraving with the word 'cat' underneath. His mother had taught him his letters and he had been reading for a year. He could not work out what Mrs Bartholomew wanted. He sat at his desk, mouth open.

That was the first time he was paddled with Mrs

Bartholomew's old hairbrush for failing to respond to a question so simple he had not thought to answer it.

He could not become interested in the multiplication tables. While the others chanted through them, impatient for the morning break, he was looking under the desk at the notebook in which he was collecting his special numbers, the ones that could not be divided by any number but themselves and one. Like him, they were solitaries.

When Mrs Bartholomew pounced on him one day and seized the notebook, he was afraid she would throw it in the fire and smack him with the hairbrush again. She looked at it for a long time and put it away in her pinny pocket.

He wanted to ask for it back. Not for the numbers, they were in his head, but for the notebook, too precious to lose.

Then Dr Adair from the Academy came to the house in Church Street. Rooke could not guess who Dr Adair was, or what he was doing in their parlour. He only knew that he had been washed and combed for a visitor, that his infant sisters had been sent next door to the neighbour woman, and that his mother and father were sitting on the uncomfortable chairs in the corner with rigid faces.

Dr Adair leaned forward. Did Master Rooke know of numbers that could be divided by nothing but themselves and one? Rooke forgot to be in awe. He ran up to his attic room and came back with the grid he had drawn, ten by ten, the first hundred numbers with these special ones done in red ink: two, three, five and on to ninety-seven. He pointed, there was a kind of pattern, do you see, here and here? But one hundred numbers was not enough, he needed a bigger sheet of paper so he could make a square twenty or even thirty a side, and then he could find the true pattern, and perhaps Dr Adair might be able to provide him with such a sheet?

His father by now had the rictus of a smile that meant his son was exposing his oddness to a stranger, and his mother was looking down into her lap. Rooke folded the grid and hid it under his hand on the table.

But Dr Adair lifted his fingers from the grubby paper.

'May I borrow this?' he asked. 'I would like, if I may, to show it to a gentleman of my acquaintance who will be interested that it was created by a boy of seven.'

After Dr Adair went, the neighbour woman brought his sisters back. She inspected Rooke and said loudly, as if he were deaf, or a dog, 'Yes, he looks clever, don't he?'

Rooke felt the hairs on his head standing up with the heat of his blush. Whether it was because he was stupid or clever, it added up to the same thing: the misery of being out of step with the world.

＊

When he turned eight Dr Adair offered the bursary. It was just words: *a place at the Portsmouth Naval Academy*. The boy thought it could not be too different from the life he knew, went along blithely and hardly waved goodbye to his father at the gate.

The first night there he lay rigid in the dark, too shocked to cry.

The other boys established that his father was a clerk who went every day to the squat stone building near the docks where the Office of Ordnance ran its affairs. In the world of Church Street, Benjamin Rooke was a man of education and standing, a father to be proud of. At the Portsmouth Naval Academy a mile away, he was an embarrassment. *A clerk! Oh dearie me!*

A boy took everything out of his trunk, the shirts and under-things his mother and grandmother had so carefully made, and hurled them through the window into the muddy yard three flights below. A man in a billowing black gown caught Rooke painfully by the ear and hit him with a cane when he tried to say that he had not done it. A big boy sat him up on a high wall out behind the kitchens and poked him with a stick until he was forced to jump down.

His ankle still hurt from the fall, but that was not the pain at his heart.

His attic in Church Street wrapped its corners and angles around him, the shape of his own odd self. At the Academy, the cold space of the bleak dormitory sucked out his spirit and left a shell behind.

Walking from the Academy back to Church Street every Saturday evening to spend Sunday at home was a journey between one world and another that wrenched him out of shape each time. His mother and father were so proud, so warm with pleasure that their clever son had been singled out, that he could not tell them how he felt. His grandmother might have understood, but he could not find the words to tell even her how he had lost himself.

When it came time for him to walk back, Anne held his hand with both hers, pulling at him with all her child's weight and crying for him to stay. She was not yet five, but somehow knew that he longed to remain anchored in the hallway. His father peeled her fingers away one by one and shooed him out the door, waving and smiling, so that Rooke had to wave too and put a grin on his face. All the way up the street he could hear Anne wailing, and his nan trying to comfort her.

Many great men had received their educations at the Academy, but no one there was excited by the numbers he learned to call primes. Nor were they interested when he showed them the notebook where he was trying to work the square root of two, or how you could play with pi and arrive at surprising results.

Rooke learned at last that true cleverness was to hide such thoughts. They became a kind of shame, a secret thing to be indulged only in private.

Conversation was a problem he could not solve. If no answer seemed necessary to a remark, he said nothing. Before he learned, he had unwittingly rebuffed several overtures.

Then it was too late.

At other times he talked too much. In response to some remark about the weather, he might wax enthusiastic about the distribution of rainfall in Portsmouth. He would share the fact that he had been keeping a record of it, that he had a jar on the windowsill on which he had scratched calibrations, of course when he was home on Sundays he took the jar with him, but the windowsill there was somewhat more exposed to the prevailing south-westerly wind than the one at the Academy and therefore got more rain. By this time whoever had commented on it being a fine day was sidling away.

He yearned to be a more ordinary sort of good fellow, but was helpless to be other than he was.

He came to hate the boastful cupola on the roof of the Academy, its proud golden globe, hated the white stone corners that hemmed in the bricks of the façade. The portico of the main doorway seemed too narrow for its grandiose columns and its miniature pediment, the door tiny in the middle like a face with eyes too close together.

Reluctantly approaching the place after a Sunday at home, still feeling Anne's hands pulling at him, Rooke would look up at the second floor where the rich boys had their rooms. If the curtains were open on the left-hand window, it meant that Lancelot Percival James, the son of the Earl of Bedwick, was in. A plump booming slow-witted boy, he had no time for a schoolfellow whose father was nothing more than a clerk and whose home did not have proper servants, only a maid-of-all-work. Even boys who fawned on Lancelot Percival were tired of hearing about his butler, his cook, his many maids and footmen, not to mention the sundry grooms and gardeners who took care of the estate, and the gamekeeper who protected the earl's pheasants from those who might try to help themselves.

Lancelot Percival lay in wait for Rooke and usually managed to give him a punch in passing, or spill ink on his precious linen shirt. The other boys watched without expression, as if it were normal, like killing a fly.

Lancelot Percival James's illustrious line was based on the sugar trade, and behind that on the islands of Jamaica and Antigua, and finally on the black slaves on those islands. Lancelot Percival did not understand why the square on the hypotenuse was equal to the sum of the squares on the other two sides, but he became eloquent on why the British Empire in general, and his own illustrious family in particular, would collapse if slavery were abolished.

Rooke puzzled about that idea as he puzzled at his primes. He had never seen a black man, so the issue was abstract, but something about the argument did not cohere. Think as he might, though, he could not find a path around Lancelot Percival's logic.

In any case, it was best to keep out of Lancelot Percival's way.

When he could, he slipped down to the water's edge at the mouth of the harbour where the Round Tower looked out to sea. There was a shingle beach at the foot of the ancient masonry where no one ever came. Its emptiness matched his own, a companion of sorts.

He had a secret slot in the wall where he kept his collection of pebbles. They were all ordinary, each valuable only for being different from the others. He whispered to himself as he crouched over them, pointing out their qualities. *Look at how this one has little dark specks in it! And do you see how that one is like the surface of the moon?*

He became his own question and his own answer.

At the Academy his only consolations were found within the pages of books. Euclid seemed an old friend. *Things that equal the same thing also equal one another. The whole is greater than the part.* In Euclid's company it was as if he had been speaking a foreign language all his life, and had just now heard someone else speaking it too.

He pored over Lily's *Grammar of the Latin Tongue,* loved the way the slippery mysteries of language could be reduced to units as reliable and interchangeable as numbers. *Dico, dicis, dicet.* Dative, genitive, ablative. He came to feel that Greek and Latin, French and German were not so much ways of speaking as machines for thinking.

Most of all, the heavens were transformed by the Academy's instruction in astronomy and navigation. It was a revelation to learn that the stars were not whimsical points of light, but part of a shape so gigantic it made Rooke dizzy. There was a cross-eyed feeling, standing on the earth and at the same time watching it from somewhere beyond. From that vantage point it was not rooms, fields, streets, but a ball of matter hurtling through space on an orbit the exact shape of which had been intuited by a German called Mr Kepler and proved by an Englishman called Mr Newton, who had a bridge named after him in Cambridge.

Rooke spent fruitless hours wishing that Euclid or Kepler were still alive to converse with him. The world they described was an orderly one in which everything had a place. Even, perhaps, a boy who seemed to have no place.

When the chaplain discovered that he had perfect pitch, it seemed another curse.

'C sharp!' he cried, and Rooke listened inside himself somewhere and sang a note. The chaplain jabbed at the piano.

'B flat, Rooke, can you give me B flat?'

Rooke listened, and sang, and the man turned to him on the piano stool, so flushed that for a shocked moment Rooke thought that he was going to kiss him. Behind him in the choir stalls his classmates snickered, and Rooke knew he would pay later.

But as soon as his legs were long enough the chaplain taught him to play the organ in the chapel. A door opened in a world that had seemed nothing but wall.

Rooke loved the logic of the notation, the way the fundamental unit of the breve could be broken into smaller and smaller pieces. Even the quickest hemi-demi-semi-quaver was part of that original breve, the sonority unheard but underlying and giving meaning to every note.

Then there was the machine itself. An organ was nothing more than dozens of tubes of air. Every pipe had just one note to sing, was incapable of any other: one pipe, one note. Each stood in its place alongside the others, its metal mouth open, full of air waiting to be moved. Sitting at the keyboard twenty yards away at the other end of the chapel, Rooke would play a chord and listen as each pipe sang out its note. He almost wept with gratitude that the world could offer such a glory of sound.

He sat in the chapel for hours picking his way through fugues. A dozen notes, hardly music. But then those few notes spoke to each other, subject and answer, by repetition, by diminution, by augmentation, even looping backwards on themselves in a course like the retrograde motion of Mars. He listened as if he had as many ears as fingertips, and, like a blind man, could feel textures that were barely there. At the end of two or three pages of music he would hear all the voices twining together in a construction of such dizzying power that the walls of the chapel could barely contain it.

Others, tiring of the sound of Buxtehude and Bach for hours on end, would complain there was no tune. That was exactly the thing he liked best about a fugue, the fact that it could not be sung. A fugue was not singular, as a melody was, but plural. It was a conversation.

On the organ bench he sat through hundreds of sermons, his back to the crowded pews, and he mumbled the morsels of bread and sipped from the chalice with the others. But the God of sin and retribution, of the mysteries of suffering and resurrection, did not speak to him. He had no argument with God, but for him God was not in those words or those rituals.

He had seen God in the night sky long before he understood its patterns. There was something about the way the body of the stars moved together as one that he had always found miraculous and comforting.

On the long winter evenings Rooke would slip outside, past the kitchens, and stand in the yard looking up. In the cold the constellations were close and brilliant. He was comforted by the way you could always find the Charioteer and the Little Bear circling the sky together. Each sparkle did not need to find its way across the darkness alone but moved together with its fellows, held fast in its place by some mighty hand.

That the moon was sometimes a sliver and sometimes a plate had seemed when he was a child to be a sly trick. But when he understood the reason, he was awed. There was a pattern, but he had been looking for it on the wrong scale. A week was not enough to see it, a month was needed.

He hoped that all understanding might be as simple as a matter of scale. If a man had not a week, not a year, not even a lifetime—if he had millennia, aeons—all the seemingly erratic movements of heavenly bodies and earthly vicissitudes would turn out to have meaning. Some kinds of order were too vast for a human to know. But below the chaos of a single human life, you could trust that a cosmic breve was sounding.

As the chaplain had his Gospels, Rooke had his own sacred text in which his God made Himself plain: mathematics. Man had been given a brain that could think in numbers, and it could not be coincidence that the world was unlocked by that very tool. To understand any aspect of the cosmos was to look on the face of God: not directly, but by a species of triangulation, because to think mathematically was to feel the action of God in oneself.

He saw others comforted by their ideas of God: as a stern but kindly father, or a brother sharing a burden. What comforted Rooke, on the contrary, was the knowledge that as an individual he did not matter. Whatever he was, he was part of a whole, one insignificant note within the great fugue of being.

That imposed a morality beyond the terse handful of commands in the chaplain's book. It was to acknowledge the unity of all things. To injure any was to damage all.

He dreamed of leaving the place, not just the Academy but Portsmouth, closed in on itself, squeezed tightly around the harbour, those narrow streets where everyone knew him too well, Benjamin Rooke's eldest, a good enough lad but a little fey.

He had no evidence, but doggedly believed that there would one day be a place, somewhere in the world, for the person he was.

In 1775 Rooke turned thirteen and Dr Adair took his talented pupil with him to Greenwich to meet his friend the Astronomer Royal.

It was further from home than Rooke had ever travelled. He spent the journey staring from the coach window at everything that passed, all as unfamiliar as darkest Africa. Every muddy hamlet was unknown, every gawping farmhand was a stranger. By the end of the day he was drunk with novelty.

Dr Vickery was a man of middle age with a heavy-jowled face and sleepy eyes that slid away. Rooke recognised that: he also found it hard to meet the eyes of another person.

He was too overwhelmed by being in the long-windowed hexagonal room where Halley had calculated the movements of his comet to respond properly to the greeting of the

Astronomer Royal. But Dr Vickery was not troubled by the boy's awkwardness. He drew him over to the wall to which was attached an enormous quarter-circle of brass, the calibrations about its edge as finely etched as the chasing on Dr Adair's gold watch.

'Master Rooke, I know you will find this quadrant of interest. Eight feet radius, and do you observe the marking of the arc plates? Done by Bird of London by the method of continual bisection.'

He shot a look at the boy, who knew about quadrants only from books and had no idea what the *method of continual bisection* might be.

'Forgive me my enthusiasm, Master Rooke. Do you know, there are days when I wait impatiently for night, unlike the rest of the human species. So much so that my wife says I must have something of the bat in my constitution!'

It was a joke, Rooke saw. The man was trying to put him at his ease. But he also thought that Mrs Vickery had put her finger on an odd and leathery quality to the man.

He was at Greenwich for two weeks and felt, for the first time in his life, that he was in the right place.

Dr Vickery showed him the mysteries of the quadrant and the Dollond telescope, let him wind one of the clocks made by Mr Harrison, its brass wings folding and stretching, folding and stretching, and the delicate ratchet advancing notch by notch. He taught him the moves of chessmen, demonstrated the dangerous power of the seemingly helpless pawn, set him the problem of the Knight's Tour to see what he could make of it.

In the Observatory library Rooke could not settle. As he read one book, another caught his eye, and then another. There was a boy at the Academy who was like that about buns, reaching for a third even while the first was in his mouth and a second in his hand.

On Dr Vickery's recommendation he tried to follow Euler's analysis of the motions of comets. He read Kepler's account of how each of his errors had cancelled out the other and revealed the truth concerning the shape of orbits. He gulped down the journal of the great Captain Cook, and wanted to read Mr Banks' account of New South Wales too, but had only time to skim the contents: *Quadrupeds—ants and their habitations—scarcity of people—implements for catching fish—canoes—language.*

At the end of his stay, Dr Vickery gripped the boy's hand and patted him on the shoulder, the two of them smiling past each other. Then he presented Rooke with a copy of his *Nautical Almanac* for 1775. He opened it at the flyleaf so Rooke could read the inscription: *To Master Daniel Rooke, an astronomer of the fairest promise.*

Two years later, just before he turned fifteen, Rooke's schooldays came to an end. He wrote to Dr Vickery hinting for a position at the Observatory, or in another observatory, anywhere he might go on watching the heavens and performing solitary calculations.

Dr Vickery had to explain that the world did not need astronomers in any great quantity. Not even the Astronomer Royal could get young Rooke an appointment. Not until some other man died.

It was never put as baldly as that, but Rooke took the point. He must look elsewhere. For a boy born into his station in life, no matter how quick to catch on to Euclid, no matter how perfect his pitch, the best prospect was not a mile from home.

He might have enlisted in the navy, but naval commissions were too dear. His Majesty's Marine Forces, Portsmouth Division, was the place for men like him: he would become a soldier of the sea. Promotion was slow, but commissions were cheaper.

Rooke knew his timing was lucky. War with the American colonies was giving the king a bottomless hunger for men, even for a studious boy who had no instinct for a fight. The Americans were daily expected to collapse. The rebels were barefoot, it was said, their guns nothing more than sticks.

Rooke showed Anne and Bessie where he was going, watching his sisters' pale soft hands turning the globe he had made out of wire and paper carefully cut and glued. Making it had been a way of passing the difficult hours of the last days before he boarded his ship. His Majesty's Marines promised a life of some sort, but waiting to start that life was an awkward time of hope and apprehension mixed, suspended between one existence and another.

'The same latitude, more or less,' he said. 'See Boston here? But quite a different longitude, of course.'

Bessie was too young even to pretend to follow, did not, in any case, have that kind of mind. At eleven, Anne wanted to think it through.

'So it will be a different time? When we are having dinner, you will be eating breakfast. If you could travel quickly enough you might have two breakfasts and two dinners!'

He put his arm around her and hugged her. He would miss his clever sister. She was the one person in the world with whom he had never needed to pretend to be someone else.

*

He was issued with the uniform, the white breeches, the red jacket with the braid and the regimental brass buttons. They gave him a musket and taught him how to load the powder and lead ball into the muzzle, ram the wadding down tight against them, pour powder into the pan to prime the charge.

It was an ingenious machine, its smooth metal parts operating by satisfying logic. The trigger caused the flint to fall, the falling flint made a spark against the striker plate, the spark caused the powder in the pan to explode and set off the charge behind the ball, propelling it along the barrel. It was as pleasing in its sequence as a sextant whose mirrors and slots told you where the sun was in the sky.

In due course he got his commission as second lieutenant and was assigned to His Majesty's ship of the line *Resolution*. As he sat in the tender watching the ship grow larger he determined that this would be a fresh start. No one knew him here: Daniel Rooke, so clever he was stupid. Along with the new red coat and the musket on its strap over his shoulder, he could put on a brand-new self.

By chance his hammock in the bowels of *Resolution* hung next to that of a man who could not have been more different from himself.

Talbot Silk was small and quick of make, his narrow face and overly thin mouth far from handsome but transformed by an eager liveliness that was hard to resist.

'Now Rooke,' he said that first afternoon, when the quartermaster had showed them their hammocks and left them to it. 'There's a good fellow, I beg you to tell me straight, are you a snorer? Because if you are, we will have to come to an arrangement.'

'Why no,' Rooke began, 'that is, I do not know, how can I know? I, well, that is, you will have to tell me whether I am or not.'

Silk gave him a wry look, had already summed up his neighbour and forgiven him.

'By Jove, Rooke, I can see that you and I will get on famously. I will stay awake tonight on purpose and let you know in the morning. Now come with me, I happen to know that there are not enough dumplings to go around tonight, so let us be Johnny-on-the-spot, eh?'

Silk was disliked by no one: he was cordial, amusing and easy, always in the right place with just the right words. It was rumoured, among the more malicious of his fellow officers, that his father was a dancing master. It was true that he was light on his feet in a conversation. He could amuse others with a droll quirk of the eyebrow and a dry tone of voice, was a storyteller who could turn the most commonplace event into something entertaining.

Silk's charm had already taken him far: only two years older than Rooke, but already first lieutenant, and with his lively eyes on the next prize. War was no more than an opportunity on the way to the creation of Captain Silk.

With Silk beside him as a model of how it was done, Rooke worked at inventing an acceptable version of himself for use in the rough camaraderie of the officers' mess. He learned how to exchange a banality or two. He steeled himself to return the gaze of others. Watching the games of cup-and-walnut that the lieutenants played on the mess table, he could see that winning was simply a matter of becoming deaf to the patter, and thought he would like to take a turn, but was too shy.

The new Daniel Rooke was not entirely unlike the old one. He was still a quiet fellow who liked to hang back in the shadows, and forgot himself so far one night as to accept the challenge of multiplying 759 by 453 in his head. At the Academy that would have opened him to mockery, but on board *Resolution* it seemed nothing worse than remarkable.

He supposed that in the little world of a ship, such a talent made him useful to know. A man standing beside a clever duffer might enjoy some reflected glory from his gifts.

At dinner in the mess, Rooke could laugh along with everyone else at Silk's description of what the bosun had said when he dropped the double block on his foot. He could turn to his neighbour and share the joke, just another lieutenant enjoying himself. After dinner he could raise his glass with all the others and join them in shouting the favourite toast of junior officers hopeful of advancement: *to war and a sickly season!*

✳

Resolution blockaded Boston Harbour and did the Atlantic run with supplies to His Majesty's forces in the colony, but for Rooke's first year aboard her she was not involved in the fighting. War was a leisurely thing, in which a young man who knew how to reckon the position of the ship by the lunar distance method and had a copy of the *Almanac* inscribed by the Astronomer Royal was useful on the quarterdeck.

Rooke supposed he should have known that a ship was a floating observatory, but it came as an unexpected gift. Not quite an astronomer, but at least a navigator, he spent his days steadying the sextant and then in the large quiet light of the

Great Cabin working through the arithmetic of longitude and latitude. On board *Resolution* his talents seemed at last to have found a home.

When the ship put into Antigua, in the Leeward Islands, for supplies, Silk was full of a scheme. Someone had told him about a certain house, at the end of a certain laneway up the hill behind English Harbour, where a group of red-blooded young British officers would be made welcome.

'Yes, you too!' he insisted. 'Think of it as part of your education if you must, Rooke, at least as important as trigonometry or Greek!'

Rooke did not take much convincing. He was glad to have an opportunity to make certain discoveries one could guess at from the shapes of one's sisters and their friends, but which he knew would never be learned except from experience.

Once ashore, Silk led the straggle of junior officers as confidently as if he had visited English Harbour and its delights a hundred times. He strode along the quay, turned left at a house with brilliant geraniums dripping red down its white wall, and went on into the heart of the town.

Everywhere Rooke saw the black faces of the slaves that Lancelot Percival had spoken of. He saw women in a muddy yard, doubled over tubs scrubbing away at laundry, shouting to each other above the splashing. He paused to listen, hearing a language like nothing he had ever heard before: not Latin, not Greek, not French, none of the languages he had studied at the

Academy, sounds as opaque to his understanding as if he were a baby. He took a few steps into the yard to hear better, but Silk shouted to him to *come along Mr Rooke, come along now, we are not here to wash our underlinen!*

As they walked through the streets he saw slaves harnessed into carts, hauling the firewood and water of the garrison. On the edge of town black men and women swayed along with huge bundles of cane or baskets full of pineapples balanced on their heads. In the fields others crouched over the squares where they planted the cane, their skin gleaming with sweat.

Even when they passed close by on the narrow streets, Rooke noticed that the slaves never looked him in the face. It must be a thing they were taught: never to look a white man in the face. Their own features were exotic, powerful, as if carved from a stronger medium than the insipid putty of English faces.

But he was shy to look too hard.

Seeing for himself a system in which a man could be bought and owned, as one might buy a horse or a gold watch, Rooke found that Lancelot Percival's abstractions about the collapse of the British Empire did not convince. The slaves were utterly strange, their lives unimaginable, but they walked and spoke, just as he did himself. That speech he had heard was made up of no sounds he could give meaning to, but it was language and joined one human to another, just as his own did.

He still did not know how to rebut Lancelot Percival's logic concerning the collapse of the British Empire, but now that he had seen the slaves he knew this: they were not the same as a horse or a gold watch.

Silk strode on, up the hill behind the port, along a narrow laneway into a hamlet of rough dwellings where hens pecked and lame dogs barked at the men in their red coats. At the end of the last stony alley, he knew which door to knock at.

The woman Rooke was given—large, handsome, brown-skinned, red-lipped—watched as he bashfully lowered his breeches. He never forgot her face, shrewd and amused, as she exclaimed, 'Bless you, boy, you are hung like a damned horse!'

Newton's calculus, the lunar distance method of determining longitude, and this other business: it was a private reassurance that he was a natural at least at a few things.

Life in His Majesty's service unspooled itself day by day in a manner he saw no reason to think would ever end. The service gave a shape to his life, allowed him to play with the brass machines and the numbers, even offered him the nearest thing to comrades that he was ever likely to have. When he thought back to the boy counting his pebbles on the beach under the Round Tower, he realised that, contrary to all his expectations, he had found a life.

*

L ike everyone else, he had taken the oath. It was easy to raise his right hand and swear that he would serve and obey. It was nothing but words.

But for the many hours of a certain long hot afternoon on the ramparts at English Harbour, he learned where those splendid words might lead. Some officers from *Renegade* had failed to serve and obey. They had not actually disobeyed, not got as far as mutiny. They had only talked about it. But it was brought home to Rooke that mere words could have the power of life and death. The leader of the mutineers—a lieutenant of marines like himself—was hanged. He opened his mouth as if to speak just as the bag was pulled down over his head. No one in the crowd breathed. Then a shout rang out, the floor fell away, and he hung jerking at the end of the rope. When he shat himself the smell travelled over the crowd. Rooke smelled it, heard the rustle among the others as they smelled it too.

Rooke willed the agonised jerking to stop. He could not look away, felt that he had to be part of it. If he looked away the wretch would go on twitching forever. The man had got a hand half free of its binding and as his body twirled on the end of the rope Rooke could see it opening and closing.

When the lieutenant was nothing more than a bag of meat within his clothes, his head kinked sideways, the crowd breathed a long sigh. Rooke tried to take a breath but a shudder came up from deep within him and he heard himself moan.

The other two men, also lieutenants, had not led, only followed, and were spared the noose. They stood, already shrunken, while their commander unsheathed his sword and struck off their badges of rank, then their regimental brass buttons, one by one. He was loose with his sword and, when he had finished, the jackets were sad wounded things, the fabric sliced, the facings flapping loose.

Then they were escorted out of the gate. Their bare heads, publicly cropped by the barber, looked undersized in the merciless light as they were sent into oblivion. Of course their hair would grow back and they would continue to walk about, and breathe and eat: they were not dead. But they might as well be. They would never again have a place in the world. No one wanted to have any dealings, personal or professional, with a man who had been ejected in dishonour.

Every officer at the garrison had stood to attention, muskets at the slope, and watched. Watching had not been a choice, because the spectacle was the whole point. No one who sweated through that pitiless stretch of time would ever forget what happened to those who did not serve and obey.

Rooke knew he would not forget. In that afternoon in which feeling had been assaulted into numbness he saw that under the benign surface of life in His Majesty's service, under its rituals and its uniforms and pleasantries, was horror.

He had thought to find a niche in which he could make a life. What was forced into his understanding that eternal burning afternoon, was that a payment would be extracted. His Majesty had no use for any of the thoughts and sensibilities and wishes that a man might contain, much less the disobedience to which he might be inspired. To bend to the king's will required the suspension of human response. A man was obliged to become part of the mighty imperial machine. To refuse was to become inhuman in another way: either a bag of meat or a walking dead man.

He thought he had found all he needed in the marines. But now he dreamed of that man's hand opening and closing on air, speaking to him of something he wished he had never learned.

*

Late in the year 1781, the French navy came to the aid of the rebels and blocked the approach to Chesapeake Bay. Rooke took his place in the waist of *Resolution* with the others. A sea battle—his first experience of active combat—seemed nothing more than a question of distance, of trajectory, of speed relative to direction. They tacked all day, working themselves into position, Line Ahead, to engage with the French, and finally drew close enough. The marines waited behind the hammocks wadded up against the rail.

Fear took everyone a different way. For Rooke it led back to his old friends the primes. Seventy-nine, eighty-three, eighty-nine, ninety-seven, one hundred and one. Beside him, Silk checked that the flint of his musket was screwed in tight. Unscrewed it, turned it over, screwed it in again. Pulled the trigger to test it.

'Buckley was with Arbuthnot in March, he told me that *Victoire* contrived to send a red-hot shot into the captain's cabin on *Intrepid*, can you imagine! Which kept rolling about and burning everything until a gallant first lieutenant—Woodford, do you know him?—took it up in his speaking trumpet and threw it overboard!'

Silk took the flint out again, blew on it, turned it over, screwed it in once more. He was talking so fast that there was a fleck of foam at the corner of his mouth. Rooke nodded, pretended to listen. It was the small kindness one man could do another.

He saw the first blast of black smoke and a gout of flame from the cannons of the French ship opposite, felt *Resolution* shake and thunder as her own cannon answered.

The firing, the reloading, the ramming, the priming, the firing again: all that was familiar from having been practised so often. The theory of it was tidy: men firing and then calmly dropping to one knee to reload. What was happening on *Resolution* bore no resemblance to that.

He thought later they should have worked it out for themselves: that the deck would become a confusion of smoke and screams, because—this had never been part of any exercise—they were being fired at as well as firing.

Behind him he heard someone make a noise, half grunt and half groan, but did not turn to see, that was what they taught you, *do not break the line*. Somewhere up towards the bow, a man was screaming, short high pulses of sound.

Blindly Rooke went through the motions of loading, ramming, priming. Stepped up to the rail and fired at the smoke across the water, stepped back, fumbled for the bag of shot, kept his head down. He would not let himself hear those screams. He obeyed the imperative of his profession, and the musket in his hand obeyed the imperative of its own workings, the flint falling, the spark leaping, the ball leaving the barrel in a blast of flame and smoke.

Above the din of the muskets and the deep percussion of the cannons, Rooke heard a long splintering aloft, and saw the end of a rope twitching down towards him. He tried to duck out of the way but it caught him across the ear and as he fell he saw a clot of sail collapse and knock down the two men on his left. He was getting to his feet again when he went sprawling sideways from a blast of violent air too loud for hearing. It was so close that it was all there was, the world sucked up into this blind vortex. *This is death*, he thought. *This is what death sounds like.*

But he was not dead, knew he was on his feet again. He looked around for Silk and the picture was fixed on his blank mind like a stain: Private Truby lying nearby, his lower part a shining inchoate mass of red, of glistening pearly surfaces, of dark gleaming stuff all seething and steaming, and Truby was trying to rise, heaving upwards with his hands on the deck, looking down to see why his arms could not get him up, pushing and pushing as if he could not understand that there was no body left, only that shambles of his own flesh and entrails gluing him to the deck.

Silk was watching Truby too, his face as expressionless as a sleeping man's. His sleeve hung in tatters and blood was running down his arm and dripping from his fingertips. Between Rooke and Silk, Private Truby went on earnestly pushing at the deck with his hands, a terrible puzzled smile on his face.

*

Rooke had no memories of the spar falling on him, giving him a blow on the crown that extinguished consciousness. *Lucky to be alive*, they told him weeks later, in the hospital at Portsmouth, but he thought death would be better than the pain in his head so bad it blacked out vision and made his guts rise into his mouth.

Or was that the memory of the deck of *Resolution* on the fifth day of September in the year 1781?

During the many months of his convalescence, Anne sat by his bed hour by hour with his hand held between both of hers on the coverlet. The pain in his skull and the remembered din of the guns were always with him, Anne's hand cradling his the only thing that kept him from slipping away.

When at last he recovered enough to leave his bed, the house grew tight-walled and airless and he took to walking: slowly, falteringly, through the lanes and crooked streets of the town. He never took the same route home, walked in wide loops rather than retrace his steps. It was *away* he needed.

Most walks ended where they had when he was a child, at the ramparts where the entrance to the port narrowed. He clambered down beside the Round Tower, hanging on now at every step like an old man.

The first time he found himself there he looked for his collection of pebbles. He knew they could not still be there after more than ten years, but when he stooped to look into the hole in the wall and found it empty he felt the tears prickle. It was the injury, he supposed, that made him feel he had lost everything, and that it was too late to find it again.

The beach was the same, and as always he had it to himself.

He sat on the cold stones, rounded by the sea to egg-like smoothness, and watched the sky, the water. Low waves gathered themselves up, glittering in hazy sun, a smooth tight-drawn surface that dropped and broke apart onto the pebbles, spotting them dark, then withdrew with an unhurried slap and rattle. Out towards the Motherbank and the Isle of Wight a band of brilliant white often lay between sea and cloud, luminous against the dark water.

His life had arrived at a point of suspension, like a fleck of dirt in a glass of water. He hung in a cold bleak space. He had thought to find a future, even found it for a time, beckoning like a tease. Now there was nothing, only this pain in his head and his heart, which had seen into the vile entrails of life and smelled the evil there.

Air flowed to and fro, water mounted and drew back under the pull of the moon as it had done for as long as there had been air and water, and as it would while air and water ever remained. He sat there, stiffening on the stones, but the pain in his head eased. A kindly trance wrapped itself around him in which time could pass.

He had retreated into some tight dry place within himself, like a periwinkle marooned above the tideline. It was enough to watch the waves crest and collapse, the distant brilliant band of light contract to a line along the horizon.

A ball of mist closed in from the sea and dusk crept over the town behind him. He forced himself upright and went through the darkening streets back to that narrow parlour and attic bedroom that were his world now.

∗

Two years after the day on *Resolution* that he tried not to remember, the war ended. *Ended* was the word people used, but everyone knew that *lost* was the one that hung behind it. That ragtag bunch of barefoot rebels had somehow defeated the might of His Majesty King George the Third. It was a humiliation that could never be mentioned. The king's soldiers and sailors did not know how to take up their lives in the shadow of the word never spoken: *defeat*.

When he met Silk near the Hard in Portsmouth Harbour, Rooke saw there had been an alteration in his friend. He could still amuse with some bit of nonsense about the day he left his cap behind in the Royal Oak. But something in him was blighted by what he had seen, and by defeat. And by the half-life of half-pay. The word he used for it was *tantalism*. There was a bitterness in the way he said it. A man on half-pay did not quite starve, but he did not properly live either.

To war and a sickly season: now Rooke understood that reckless toast too well. The self that had laughed and raised his glass and shouted out the words with the others seemed to him now to be foolishly, dangerously, disastrously innocent.

Something had shifted in the friendship between Rooke and

Silk. They had both watched Private Truby wondering why he could not get up, and that had forged a bond deeper than mere good fellowship.

There on the Hard, on that day of cold glum cloud, they did not mention that monstrous thing, but wrung each other's hands so hard it hurt.

Silk was returning to his home in Cheshire. Looking at his pinched face, Rooke did not ask whether it was true his father was a dancing master.

When his health returned sufficiently, Rooke eked out his half-pay with a little tutoring of dullards in mathematics and astronomy, Latin and Greek, fuming with irritation at their slowness. Anne would come into the parlour when they left and see him glowering into the fire. She never sighed and sympathised the way his mother did. *Oh Dan*, she would cry, *what was the point of being hit on the head, if it did not give you the blessing of being as stupid as the rest of us?*

He would offer her the poker and suggest she might hit him again, until the desired effect was arrived at, and thanked God for such a sister.

But in the mornings he would wake up in the attic room under the shingles, in the bed that had only ever been meant for a child, and think of the wasted time behind him, and the years stretching ahead: he was twenty-three, and how could he ever again find a life?

D aniel Rooke was a boy collecting pebbles when Cook
had landed in New South Wales, a place almost as far
on the globe as you could travel in any direction
without starting to come back. Its remoteness was turning out to
be its greatest asset. His Majesty had formed the view that New
South Wales was ideally suited to swallow the overflow from his
prisons.

Midway through 1786, when Rooke was twenty-four, Dr
Vickery wrote to him suggesting that the proposed expedition
might have need of an astronomer. Rooke did not hesitate,
replied the same day.

To Major Wyatt, the commander of Rooke's regiment—an
irritable man whose small knowing eyes missed nothing—Dr
Vickery explained why an astronomer, along with the prisoners

and the marines, should go to New South Wales. He predicted, he told Wyatt, that the comet of 1532 and 1661 would return in the year 1788. This would be as significant an event as the return predicted by Dr Halley of the comet now named after him. However, unlike Halley's Comet, the one predicted by Dr Vickery would be visible only from the Southern Hemisphere. The Royal Observatory would be prepared to supply Lieutenant Rooke with instruments, if Major Wyatt would exempt him from ordinary duties.

Rooke suspected that Major Wyatt was probably not entirely convinced of the significance of the comet of 1532, and had only the sketchiest notion of who Dr Halley might have been. But Wyatt was not prepared to argue with the Astronomer Royal.

Rooke reminded himself that New South Wales was a smooth page waiting to be written on. *Quadrupeds, birds, ants and their habitations*: for the sixteen years since the visit by *Endeavour* they had gone about their business under the antipodean sun. Now he was being offered the chance to see them, and to be perhaps the only astronomer to record the return of Dr Vickery's comet.

Ten years before, Rooke knew he would have felt such an opportunity no more than his due. He had been blessed with intelligence, and this prospect offered him the chance to use it. It would have seemed the way things ought to be, one piece of the smooth machinery of the world moving in harmony with another.

Now he did not trust that machine. He did not think he ever would again. Life might promise, but he knew now that while it gave it also took.

Of course he would go to New South Wales. In some faraway place within him where eagerness still smouldered, he even looked forward to it. He bought notebooks and ledgers and experienced the first pulse of pleasure he had felt for a long time, running a hand over the blank leaves that he would fill with the data of this unknown land: the weather, the stars, perhaps the *quadrupeds* and even the *habitations of ants*.

Silk's letter to Rooke, urging him to volunteer, had arrived by the same mail as Dr Vickery's. Between the lines of the letter Rooke felt the new life breathed into his friend by this windfall. He had already volunteered and already been promoted. First Lieutenant Silk was now Captain-Lieutenant Silk. But rank was no longer the extent of his ambition. *Mr Debrett of Piccadilly has promised me,* Silk wrote. *'Whatever you can give us from New South Wales, we will publish.' Those were his words, and I do not intend to disappoint him!*

Silk was no more a soldier than he was himself, Rooke saw. He too had been marking time, waiting for his vocation to become possible. Rooke realised that when Silk told those stories in the mess it was not simply to entertain. For Silk, the making of the tale—the elegance of its phrases, the flexing of its shape—was the point of the exercise. The instinct to rework an event, so that the telling became almost more real than the thing itself—that had been born in Silk the way the pleasures of manipulating numbers had been born in Rooke.

I will not take no for an answer, Silk wrote.

∗

Anne had kept the globe he had made when he was fourteen. It was dusty and something had spattered against South America, but it still rotated.

'The night sky is different there,' he said. 'See the way the earth is tilted? I will see stars there that we never see from here.'

He watched her thinking it through.

'The moon, you will still see the moon? But upside down?'

She was unsure, he could tell, and was afraid of disappointing him with her stupidity. She was not stupid, only clever enough to recognise the limits of what she understood.

Outside, the rain whispered on and on, a voice just beyond the range of hearing. He got up and went around behind her, putting his hands on her shoulders and feeling the warmth of her against his chest. She spun the tremulous little globe around and around.

'I will look at the moon every night,' she said, 'and think of you looking at it too.'

He could see something droll occur to her as she turned to look up at him.

40

'Of course, so that I can see it just as you will, I shall be obliged to stand on my head, but that, my dear and esteemed brother, is a difficulty I am prepared to confront!'

When he took out the red jacket again for the first time he felt a swell of nausea. He could smell in its fabric the sweat of his terror, thought he could smell the gunpowder. He put it on, though—a new jacket would be too great an extravagance—and breathed deep to accustom his nose to being a soldier again.

He had come close to dying. Within half an inch, they had said. But he had been spared, and now this thing was being offered. What it meant he did not know, but he was willing to accept that this was the orbit his life was intended to follow.

PART TWO

The Astronomer

Begin *as you mean to go on,* Rooke's father had always told
him, so Rooke made sure he was conspicuously an
astronomer on board *Sirius.* He did not have to pretend.
By the time he had made his sextant observations, compared
them with the figures Captain Barton and Lieutenant Gardiner
had got and worked out the average, that was already a goodly
space of the afternoon. Then the geometry of latitude and
longitude began. It could not be hurried.

As captain of the fleet's flagship, Barton was wary at first
of this young soldier who thought he could navigate. His face
fell naturally into alarming sternness, so that Rooke thought
he would be ordered off the quarterdeck like an upstart. But
Barton's sternness hid a kindly heart, and when he saw
Rooke's abilities he forgave him for being a lieutenant in the

marines rather than the navy.

Lieutenant Gardiner had been Barton's right-hand man for three years, and was the officer to whom he had always turned in the past for a second set of observations. In Gardiner's position, another officer might have resented Rooke. But Gardiner, a burly sunburnt sailor, was big in every sense, everything about him on a generous scale.

On their first meeting he enfolded Rooke's hand in his own and looked square into his face. 'Welcome, Mr Rooke. Three of us on the job, the ocean might as well be the king's highway!'

The men braced themselves against the pitching of the ship, squinting into their sextants. At each reading the numbers they got were never quite the same. That was the nature of the job. But Barton and Gardiner did not cling jealously to theirs, as Rooke had seen navigators do on *Resolution*, as if the numbers on a piece of brass were a measure of manhood. Gardiner flirted with the sun as it slipped in and out of cloud, shouting at her to *show yourself, my beauty, none of this modesty!* He was always ready to assure Barton that Rooke had charmed her with a superior steadiness of hand and eye. *She is a tease, sir, and today it is Mr Rooke she favours.*

While Rooke travelled on the flagship, Silk was at the rear of the eleven ships, on board *Charlotte*. Rooke saw him only when the ships put in to various ports on the way south.

'Damned unfortunate,' Silk said when they met on the quay at Rio.

'Unlucky,' Rooke agreed, keeping to himself the thought that he enjoyed the straightforward company of the navy men, even though they did not have such art with the turn of a phrase.

Silk was pulling a worn notebook out of his pocket.

'I have made a start with my narrative, Rooke, listen to this, I am referring to Captain Cook's report of having nosegays thrown at him by young ladies here. *We were so deplorably unfortunate as to walk every evening before their balconies without being honoured with a single bouquet, though nymphs and flowers were in equal and great abundance.* Now tell me frankly, Rooke, as a friend, what do you think?'

'Very clever, very deft of phrasing,' Rooke said. 'But have you really walked there every evening?'

'Ah, Rooke the man of science! Let us call it poetic licence, my friend.'

It was foreign to Rooke, the idea of taking the real world as nothing more than raw material. His gift lay in measuring, calculating, deducing. Silk's was to cut and embellish until a pebble was transformed into a gem.

*

Captain Barton set the fleet's course but above Barton was the commodore, in whose hands all decisions finally rested. James Gilbert was an angled sort of man, all elbows and shoulders at different heights, a slight figure who took cautious steps on the sloping deck, and always that tilt to his thin body, and the sour look on his face. On board *Sirius* Rooke never saw the commodore's mouth bend into any but the most formal of smiles.

Of course the commodore's joylessness might have been the pain in his side rather than his temperament. *It is always with him, to a greater or lesser degree,* the surgeon had told them in the mess. *The kidneys, in my view, or perhaps the gall bladder.* Surgeon Weymark loved to eat and laugh, a tall man carrying an enormous belly before him like a figurehead, but there was compassion under his bonhomie. He tried every potion on the commodore, bled him and cupped him and palpated his side for an hour each morning to try to dislodge the pain, and was troubled that none of it had any effect.

When the commodore joined his officers on the quarterdeck, Gardiner went quiet and Barton's face folded down into professional severity. Rooke reminded himself what unremitting pain did to the look on one's face, but James Gilbert was a man it was difficult to warm to, sharing nothing of his thoughts with other men.

Each day at noon during the months at sea, the commodore and Captain Barton, with Rooke following respectfully behind in his capacity as astronomer, made their way together down the ladders. In the belly of the ship was a cabin guarded night and day by a sentinel. As the men approached, the sentinel moved aside to let them enter the only place in this crowded ship that was not full of bags and barrels and things folded and bound.

On a table screwed to the floor of this empty cabin, in a box screwed to the table, snug between two red silk cushions, lay the timekeeper made by Mr Kendall.

It was a package of Greenwich time that would travel with them, inviolate as a pea in a pod, all the way around the globe. When it was darkest night in New South Wales, the timekeeper would still be striking noon at Greenwich.

In its inner workings Mr Kendall's timekeeper was the descendant of the brass insect slowly beating its wings that Dr Vickery had shown Rooke as a boy, but in shape this one was like any pocket watch, except that it was the size of a soup plate. It was a nice bit of wit on the part of the watchmaker, Rooke thought, to have made this gigantic thing as if it could be hung from some colossal waistcoat pocket.

With Barton and Rooke standing close by in case the ship lurched, the commodore lifted the timekeeper out of its nest and removed the pair-case, revealing the busy secretive mechanism within, the wheels twitching time forward tooth by tooth. He took the winding key from its slot in the box, inserted it into the hole in the back of the workings, and turned it. Then he replaced the case and slipped the thing back between its cushions.

As the regulation stipulated, the sentinel was called in and each of the men told him in turn: *The timekeeper has been wound.* When the sentinel had heard the words from each of them— and only then—he moved aside from the door and allowed them to leave.

The rigmarole was wonderfully droll, Rooke thought. If he had seen it, Silk would have had the mess highly entertained, imitating the way Rooke solemnly mouthed: *The timekeeper has been wound* to the wooden-faced sentinel who had already been told it twice.

There was another thing about the ritual of the winding. Rooke was the lowliest sort of officer, a man of no importance. But during those few minutes in the cabin, rank was nothing. For that time, the astronomer Rooke was the equal of the commodore himself.

In fine weather, the whole business was redundant. But when sextants could not find the sun or moon in cloud, or the ship pitched too wildly to fix a sighting, the timekeeper, still faithfully telling the time in Greenwich even after months at sea, might be all that protected them from being dashed to pieces on the rocks of New South Wales.

*

Botany Bay proved itself immediately impossible as a place of settlement, so the commodore directed the fleet a few miles further north. It had taken nearly nine months to arrive at New South Wales: what could such a short distance further matter?

From the sea it looked as though the commodore had made a mistake. Rooke and Gardiner leaned on the rail watching as *Sirius* skewed to port and led the fleet towards what seemed no more than a notch in a high yellow cliff. They heard the sheets rattle in the blocks as the sails were slanted and *Sirius* headed for the maelstrom of white water at its base.

But the commodore had not been mistaken. Beyond the cliff an enormous body of quiet water curved away to the west. *Sirius* glided past bays lined with crescents of yellow sand and headlands of dense forest. There was something about this vast hidden harbour—bay after perfect bay, headland after shapely headland—that put Rooke in a trance. He felt he could have travelled along it forever into the heart of this unknown land. It was the going forward that was the point, not the arriving, the water creaming away under the bow, drawn so deeply along this crack in the continent that there might never be any need to stop.

As *Sirius* rounded a rocky island, Rooke saw men running along the shore, shaking spears. He could hear them on the wind calling the same word over and over: *Warra! Warra!* He did not think that they were calling *Welcome! Welcome!* He suspected a polite translation might be something like *Go to the Devil!*

With a rumbling rattle and splash the anchor was let go. When Rooke looked again, the men had gone.

They were anchored at the mouth of a small cove, sheltered by high ridges on either side. At the head of the bay was a slip of sand where a stream flowed into the cove. Behind it a shallow wooded valley ran back into the country.

The sailors readied the cutter for the shore party. A sergeant and four armed privates climbed down, then the commodore and Captain Barton. Surgeon Weymark, with an ease surprising in such a big man, followed. Rooke did not wait to be invited, but climbed down after him. He did not want to miss the chance of being among the first to step onto this place, that might have been Saturn for all anyone knew of it.

On the sand at the head of the cove Rooke felt the ground tilt under him. He snuffed up lungfuls of the air: dry, clean, astringent, sweet and sour both at once, warm and complicatedly organic after all those many weeks of nothing but the blank wind of the sea.

Weymark took a step that the ground rose up to meet and laughed so his belly shook. He was just starting to say something when they saw five native men step out of the bushes fringing the sand. From behind him in the boat, Rooke heard a series of small sounds that he knew were made by muskets being put up to shoulders.

'Steady, steady now,' he heard the sergeant say, his voice tight.

The men were dark and naked, their faces shadowed in the sunlight. *Natives,* Rooke thought, *I am face to face with natives!*

They were strange and ordinary at once: men, like himself in essence, the same shoulders and knees and private parts, although theirs were not private. A muscular grey-bearded man stood at the head of the group, the others behind him, each holding a wooden shield and spear. They watched, densely black in the sunlight.

'The trinkets, sergeant, where are the trinkets?'

The commodore turned back to the boat, reaching impatiently for the bag the sergeant handed him. He shook a string of beads so it caught the sun.

'Come, my friends,' he called. 'Look, I wager you have never seen this before!'

Even his pinched face was creased with excitement. For the first time, Rooke could see the eager boy he must once have been.

Weymark went one better, made a looking-glass flash.

'Look, sir,' he cried. 'I will let you have it for your very own, if only you will come close enough to take it! By Jove they are cautious, Barton, look at them like a cat that wants the cream but fears the milkmaid!'

He laughed his tremendous laugh, and Rooke thought that made the men braver. The grey-haired one took a step forward.

'Yes, that's the way, Mister Darkie, come, come!'

The surgeon did a ponderous little jig and the man took a fresh grip on his spears.

In front of his sailors Barton could not caper the way Weymark was doing, but he had a string of beads too and was twirling it.

'Rooke, lad, get yourself some trinkets and try your luck!' he called.

Rooke picked out a looking-glass and walked a few steps

towards the nearest native, a man perhaps his own age, whose eyes darted from Rooke to Barton and back again, as flighty as a greyhound.

Rooke held up a hand.

'Good afternoon!'

It was like tossing a stone into a bush and wondering what bird would fly out.

This man was well made, his chest sculpted with muscle, his bearing very straight. His chest was marked with a neat pattern of raised scars, the skin decorated like a garment.

He glanced at Rooke, his mouth ajar as if to speak, the whites of his eyes stark in the blackness of his skin. In one quick movement he stepped forward, took the looking-glass and stepped back. He showed it to the man beside him and they murmured over it.

Then they lost interest. The man dropped the looking-glass on the sand, as casually as a boy in Portsmouth might let go the core of an apple. They all moved a few steps backwards and seemed to wait.

For some better gift? Some other gesture?

Weymark decided the next move. Perhaps he thought of it as entertainment, of a piece with the looking-glasses and the beads. He went boldly to the eldest of the men, a wiry grey-haired fellow, took his shield—*just to borrow*, he tried to explain by signs—and propped it up in the sand. He loaded his pistol, aimed from a short distance, cocked the hammer and fired. The native men jumped back from the explosion.

The smoke floated away. A smell of gunpowder filled the air.

The shield was a solid thing, a slab of wood two feet long and a good inch thick, but the ball had gone clean through it and left a ragged hole and a long split top to bottom. The old man picked it up. In his hands it fell into two pieces and he fitted them back together and touched with long fingers at where the ball had burst through the wood. He held the shield up against his belly and gestured, would it do the same thing to him?

'Oh my very word, yes, my black friend,' Weymark cried encouragingly. 'Split you from skull to arsehole, by God!'

Weymark thought it a fine joke, and so did Captain Barton, and by a kind of contagion Rooke laughed too.

The black men were not entertained. They frowned and spoke to each other urgently.

'Upon my word, Weymark,' the commodore called. 'You have frightened them now, what were you thinking?'

But the surgeon was untroubled. 'Well, sir, if they do not care for my exhibition of sharp-shooting, perhaps they would prefer a little music, they will find I am a man of multitudinous talents.'

Pursing up his lips, he began to whistle. Only the surgeon, Rooke thought, could be so casual with the commodore, but when a man had palpated your side day after day you would perhaps allow him a certain liberty.

It seemed that the natives did not like the surgeon's music any more than they had enjoyed his performance with the pistol. Their faces were stony. After a minute they took the two pieces of shield and disappeared into the woods.

The small bay soon had a name: Sydney Cove. It seemed made according to a different logic from the world Rooke knew. There were trees, as there were in other places, but each was stranger than the last. Some were mops, with a bare pole for a trunk and a bush of foliage twenty feet above the ground. Gnarled pink monsters twisted arthritic fingers into the sky. The squat white trees growing by the stream were padded with bark that flaked in soft sheets like paper.

Red parrots sidled along branches, chattering and whistling. Could they be taught to talk, he wondered, or learn a tune, like the one old Captain Veare had in his parlour in Portsmouth? Catching one would be the first difficulty. The birds watched him sideways, cannily. Birdlime, or a net. He had no birdlime, no net. And he could whistle a tune for himself, although he had to admit that there was something about these woods of New South Wales that made a man fall silent.

Buxtehude seemed another species here, the dialogue of a fugue from another world.

Even the rocks were not like any others he had seen, monstrous plates and shards piled haphazardly on each other. How might he describe them to Anne? Thinking of her face, the look she had as she listened to him—her head tilted, her eyes watching him, patient while he found words—he remembered the French pastry he had eaten with her at the teashop in St George's Street a few days before the fleet sailed. Layers of pastry interleaved with layers of custard, it was somewhat along the same lines as the stony parts of this landscape.

It had been impossible to eat, the custard squirting out at each mouthful. He and Anne had begun by being embarrassed but ended by laughing at each other's efforts. *My dear Anne, I find myself in a land remarkably like the pastry we had that day at Pennycook's, that needed to be eaten in private, in other respects it is a dry and stony place.*

He pictured her reading it in the little parlour. He hoped it would make her smile.

*

Within a day of the fleet dropping anchor, the work parties of prisoners had begun to hack at the bushes and trees. Two weeks later the head of the cove was a clutter of bleeding timber, scraped yellow earth and tents that tilted and sagged. As soon as a large enough piece of ground was cleared, the population was assembled for the commodore to address it.

He was given a sea-chest to stand on in the shade of a sprawling tree and the prisoners were herded onto the rocky ground in front of him. They shuffled and muttered, indifferent to the significance of the moment. The redcoats made a ragged circle around them. In round numbers, eight hundred prisoners, two hundred marines. Now that they were off the ships, it seemed to Rooke that the mathematics of control were precarious.

Major Wyatt, his thrust-out jaw making him look somewhat like a carp, stood in a blaze of gold braid. His face was tilted up towards the commodore beside him on the chest, but Rooke could see his eyes flicking, watching the prisoners. He had distributed the three captains of marines at equal distances around the perimeter of the crowd. Rooke saw Silk, somehow contriving to stand at attention while looking as relaxed as a man about to step into a dance. Rooke had not met Captain Gosden until they landed in New South Wales, but he thought the man should never have been accepted for the expedition. His face was pouchy, pale but for hectic spots high on his cheeks, and it cost him a visible effort to hold himself straight. As usual he had his handkerchief in his hand and the preoccupied gaze of a man trying not to cough. Silk had amused Rooke by describing the third captain, Lennox, as a human string bean. Lennox and his musket stood together, two long thin military machines waiting to do their duty.

Rooke sweated into his red jacket. The humid air held the heat and the blue sky beat down headachy light. He could feel his eyes squinting against it, envied Gilbert in his patch of shade.

Barton and Gardiner and the other naval officers had come ashore in their best blue coats for the ceremony and stood watching. They were simply onlookers. They would sail away again before long. For a moment Rooke wished that he were one of them.

When Wyatt shouted his order Rooke adopted the regulation stance for the salute, musket against his shoulder, left foot forward. As he pulled his finger back against the trigger and braced himself for the noise, he had a moment's nausea.

The volley of shots rang out, a little more ragged than Major Wyatt would no doubt have liked. A flock of big white parrots erupted out of a tree nearby. They heeled and flapped over the humans gathered by the stream, making harsh metallic noises somewhat in sympathy with the ringing that the gunfire had awoken in Rooke's head.

He lowered the musket and stood it upright beside him. How happy he would be if today, the seventh of February 1788, were the last time he ever fired it.

The commodore strained himself upright on his box, shouting to make himself heard against the parrots. He read aloud his commission from King George the Third in which, between one word and the next, James Gilbert became monarch by proxy. Like His Majesty, the brand-new governor of New South Wales had been granted the power of life and death over his subjects.

Every time Governor Gilbert uttered the name of His Majesty, from some anonymous place within the restless mass of prisoners there was the unmistakable sound of a hawk and spit.

The white parrots flew off and there was silence in the little valley. On behalf of His Majesty, the governor proclaimed sovereignty over the territory called New South Wales, and for the first time it was given a shape and size. North to south it extended between latitude ten degrees thirty-seven minutes and latitude forty-three degrees forty-nine minutes. East to west it contained all the land between where they presently stood and one hundred and thirty-five degrees of longitude east.

Rooke applied his mind to some interesting mental arithmetic. Thirty-three degrees of latitude was a distance north to south of over two thousand miles. Sixteen degrees of longitude represented about eight hundred miles east to west. At a rough estimate, His Majesty had just acquired a plot double the size of France, Spain and Germany combined.

Governor Gilbert was still reading. 'The natives are on all occasions to be treated with amity and kindness,' he shouted above the increasing swell of sound from the prisoners.

Some small object flew out of the middle of the crowd towards him and fell into a bush nearby.

'It is of the utmost importance to open friendly intercourse with them,' he pressed on. 'Without their cooperation, the progress and even the existence of this colony will be threatened. His Majesty has instructed me to establish good relations with the greatest possible despatch, and to become familiar with the native tongue as swiftly as opportunity may make possible.'

This was an aspect of New South Wales that Rooke had not considered: the colony needed an astronomer but it might also need a linguist. It was true that, in the two weeks since the day of beads and looking-glasses, the natives had appeared only once or twice, and then fleetingly. Rooke had been on board each time and not seen them. He had glimpsed figures across the port on the opposite shore, smoke rising from various distant points, and canoes silhouetted against the bright water. But so far there had been no opportunity to show the natives *amity and kindness*.

It seemed to Rooke that the governor was hurrying to bring the assembly to a close.

'I ask that you kneel with me now,' he cried. 'The reverend will give thanks on behalf of us all, kindly step up Mr Pullen.'

From the crowd a female voice guffawed. 'Thanks! Thanks for what?'

He thought he recognised the voice of a handsome foul-mouthed woman who, off Rio, had been dunked in the sea to quieten her. She set them all off now, the prisoners on their feet shouting and whistling, threatening to overrun the line of marines.

Rooke steeled himself to do his duty, but Wyatt spoke to Lennox with a twitch of an eyebrow, and Lennox waded into the crowd. The prisoners must have been familiar with the captain. Lennox had only to lay about him briefly with the butt of his gun and they subsided, so that Rooke was not obliged to do any more than grip his musket and look alert.

But there would be other times, he thought, endless other times when every man in a red coat would be required to act. On the voyage he had established his distinction from the other marines. He must continue as he had begun. The western headland of the cove had a high remote look that might suit an observatory, and would certainly suit a man who had no wish to play the part of prison guard. He would investigate it as soon as he could and make sure that Lieutenant Rooke was seen to be too busy with the celestial bodies for any terrestrial duty.

The reverend was up on the box now, unwinding his usual endless flowery prayer. For his homily he had taken a line from Psalms: *What shall I render unto the Lord for all His benefits toward me?* Rooke thought it might have been especially selected to provoke a congregation of men and women who had no choice about being in a place where benefits promised to be thin on the ground. The governor's face was entirely without expression as he listened, but Rooke thought he saw more tightness than usual in his narrow jaw.

When the reverend paused for a breath the governor was ready.

'Amen,' he announced, and Pullen was obliged to move on to the benediction.

The assembly dispersed, the work parties were chivvied back to their axes and picks. Rooke slipped away, avoiding the eye of anyone who might call, *Oh, Lieutenant Rooke, might I trouble you to give me some assistance here?* To get to that promising headland, though, he had to pass the space being cleared on the western side of the stream. Major Wyatt referred to it as the parade ground, although as yet it was nothing more than a slope of grey dirt bristling with stumps.

Walking briskly, as if on some urgent errand, Rooke heard the major's unmistakable roar and saw him out of the corner of his eye, red-faced with heat and rage, step over to a prisoner. He prodded him hard between the shoulderblades so the wretch hefted his axe and squared up to a tree, and the others bent to their inept chopping and chipping. One tall fellow in a suit of striped slops much too small for him—the trousers up around his calves, the sleeves almost at his elbows, the jacket gaping open on his massive chest—dabbed at the ground with his pick. He was moving fast enough to avoid Wyatt's stick, but making no impact on the stump he was attacking.

Next to him a man with the hollow cheeks of toothlessness grubbed away at another stump. Rooke saw how each blow of his pick struck a root and bounced but the man did not try another spot, lifting the pick, bringing it down, taking the recoil in his scrawny arms.

Stupidity, Rooke wondered, or indifference? For Major Wyatt, the grubbing-out of a stump was a step on the way to a parade ground. For this man, it must be a task as pointless, as punitive, as the treadmill in the prison he had been plucked from.

Thank God for astronomy, he thought, and kept walking.

It seemed he was not the only officer keeping out of the way of duties. Away from the work parties, Silk was sitting on a rock scribbling in a notebook and smiling to himself. When he saw Rooke he moved over hospitably.

'*The natives seemed at a loss to know of what sex we were,*' he read aloud, '*which having understood, they burst into the most immoderate fits of laughter.* You missed that encounter, Rooke, but is it not entertaining in the greatest degree? We had one of the sailors give a visual demonstration of the truth—by chance an individual supremely equipped for the task. The natives were so astonished that I am sorry to say they vanished again soon after. My puzzle now is to keep the humour of that extraordinary encounter while finding the words for it which will not bring a blush to a maiden's cheek.'

'Yes, excellent,' Rooke said, thinking *I hope Silk does not put me in his book.* But Silk did not hear any reservation in his friend's praise.

'Odd, though, is it not, that the natives are avoiding us? Gardiner told me that they approached him in the fishing boat yesterday. He gave them some fish, but they did not stay to chat.'

'Word must have travelled. Of the impressive equipment, you know, of the other man.'

But Silk had finished with that joke. 'Rooke, my friend, will you be good enough to help me?'

'Help you?'

'I do not mean with the writing, no. But I will not be able to be everywhere at once. There will be things you hear of, which I will miss. I look to you as a friend.'

He touched Rooke's arm.

'Will you do that, old fellow? Will you help me make my narrative a sparkling gem of a thing before which Mr Debrett will bow down in praise?'

Rooke was surprised by the nakedness of the appeal. He had never seen anything matter to Silk. Nothing—except, perhaps, Private Truby on the deck of *Resolution*—was more than material for an anecdote.

He saw that for Silk, as for himself, New South Wales was not simply four years of full pay and the chance of advancement, and that evading the more unsavoury duties of their profession was not the only imperative. For Silk, as for himself, the place promised other riches. New South Wales was part of a man's destiny.

✳

S hipboard life did not prepare a man for scrambling up a hillside that was like a French pastry, and halfway up the promontory on the west side of the cove, Rooke paused. It was partly to catch his breath but partly to look down at where *Sirius*, his home for most of the past year, was already a miniature below him.

He heard the ship's bell over the glaring water: quaver crotchet, quaver crotchet, quaver crotchet, quaver. Seven bells. Half past three. The timekeeper on board would be showing half past five in the morning.

The clock on the mantelpiece in the parlour at Church Street would be showing the same time. The room would be dark, clenched tight with the dank chill of late winter. In this hard empty light and breathless heat it was difficult to believe.

Upstairs everyone would be asleep under heaped blankets. Anne would be curled under his eiderdown in the attic. *I will keep it warm for you,* she had promised. *And undertake to return it, on condition that you come back safe.*

For an instant he felt it: just how far he was from home.

He was weary at the thought of the officers' mess on *Sirius* and yet another evening meal there. All those faces were known too well, and the voices that could only utter words he had heard ten dozen times before. In the congestion of the ship he had perfected the art of creating a bubble of mathematics that no one quite dared to burst. Until there were enough tents and huts he would have to continue to live on board. But an astronomer was obliged to be close to his instruments at all hours of the night, so as soon as he could he would remove to the promontory.

From the end of the point the view was worth the climb. To the east the bright waters of the harbour went out towards the sea, serrated by so many headlands, so many inlets, a few islands. To the west were more headlands, more inlets, more islands.

Just before the end of the ridge dropped away to the water there was a level place about the size of Major Wyatt's parade ground, backed by a low cliff. No trees obscured the sky. The Royal Observatory at Greenwich must once have been just such a high open hilltop.

As a crow might fly, the settlement was less than a mile

distant, but this spot felt remote. Rooke could not see the encampment, only hear the distant clunk of axes and the occasional shout. The person he was among those people—Second Lieutenant Rooke, good with numbers although inclined to be awkward with people—was someone he inhabited like a stiff suit of clothes. To stand here, where the solitude without matched the solitude within, was to be unburdened.

A man on this promontory would be part of the settlement, but not in it. Present, but forgotten. Astronomy would make a convenient screen for a self that he did not choose to share with any of the other souls marooned along with him.

The wind had fallen away. The western horizon was sliding up to meet the sun, making the port a sheet of soft gold patched with the shapes of headlands and islands.

Rooke was turning to go back to the settlement when he realised that he was being watched. Two native men were standing a short distance away, as still as the rocks, men whose dark skin made them part of the landscape. They were not looking at him but out at the water.

He remembered the men he had greeted on the first day, and the way they had reacted to Surgeon Weymark's pistol. Rooke thought its power might have been more eloquent than Weymark intended.

This seemed another chance.

'Good afternoon! Good afternoon!'

He took a few steps towards them.

'I am pleased to meet you!'

That was absurd, but at least it was words.

One man shifted the spear in his hand fractionally. Neither of the natives acknowledged by the slightest flicker of expression that a man was calling out that he was pleased to meet them.

When they began to move towards him, he thought that they were responding at last. They were not. They walked past, an arm's length away, for all the world as if he were invisible.

Hoy, he thought of saying. *Hoy, I am here, you know!* He even opened his mouth to speak, rehearsing the tone he would try for: amused, light, cheerful. But something about the dignified way they walked kept him silent.

Where the rocks dropped away to the water, the two men stepped down. Rooke could see that they had no sense of deliberating how to descend, thinking this way or that way? Their path was as familiar to them as Rooke's had been beside the Round Tower.

He went to the edge and looked down. One of the men was lying on a rock with his face almost in the water, spear over his shoulder. The other had waded in knee-deep and, as Rooke watched, he darted his spear with a movement too quick to see and held it up with a shining fish flapping on the prongs. He flipped it off, broke its spine in his hands and tucked it into the cord around his hips. Rooke was ready to give a congratulatory wave. But the man only bent back towards the water.

Why had he not spoken up when they passed so close? A

different sort of fellow—Gardiner for instance, or Silk—would not have let himself be ignored. Silk would be down there with them on the rocks, trying his hand with a spear, probably, and taking notes.

When they came back up he would not be shy. He would stand in their way until they stopped and would offer them something, his handkerchief perhaps. *Good afternoon*, he would say again, right into their faces. They would not be able to pretend no one was there. *Good afternoon*, he would say, and hold out the handkerchief. *Would you care to accept this?*

But as he continued to watch the men, they moved around the point towards the next bay and out of sight without once glancing up.

*

Rooke was taken aback when the governor resisted the idea of him establishing an observatory.

'The stars will have to wait, Mr Rooke,' he snapped. 'Dr Vickery will understand that we have more urgent matters to attend to here.'

Rooke watched his brows drawing together, creating two deep grooves. He had not prepared for this. On *Sirius*, he had been an astronomer, alongside the governor in the cabin with Mr Kendall's timekeeper, but on land he had to recognise that things were different.

'Hear me on this, Lieutenant: I have more than a thousand souls for whom I am responsible, and so far nothing but a few tents to offer them by way of shelter.'

The governor was turning away.

'But, sir, you will remember that the Astronomer Royal has provided instruments. On the basis that they will be used in the furtherance of science. In particular the comet which Dr Vickery has predicted later this year. Which he considers of the highest degree of importance.'

The governor seemed as surprised as Rooke at this fluent speech and looked at him dourly.

'I would not wish to take issue with the Astronomer Royal. That is certainly true. But why so far, Lieutenant? My wish is that the settlement remain compact, for the security of all its members. Until we can establish an intercourse with the natives we have no way of knowing their intentions.'

He was turning away again, but Rooke could not yield. He must have that lonely headland. Desperation gave his mind wings, his mouth words.

'With the greatest respect, sir.' That was a useful phrase he had heard Silk use with the governor to good effect. 'An observatory must be in a position of perfect darkness. For its best operation. As you would know.'

This was two kinds of lie, the first being *as you would know*. The governor, an adequately competent navy man, knew enough of the night sky to get a ship from one place to another, but nothing whatever of the needs of an astronomer. And the business of *perfect darkness*: well, that was at best a half-truth. The fires and flickering lamps of the settlement would hardly interfere with anyone's view of the stars.

Rooke watched the governor's narrow face: peevish but thoughtful. He was about to use his authority and simply forbid.

'In addition, sir,' Rooke said quickly, hoping that some further argument would come to him as he spoke. 'In addition, sir, the calculations are difficult. Particularly regarding a comet. For someone of my abilities. Limited abilities.'

Rooke could hear how his words laboured. He sometimes thought that he arrived at a sentence the way other people did multiplication: the hard way, by adding. He felt himself colouring but floundered on. 'Distraction, sir, distraction will tax my powers. To the limit. Solitude and quiet will be essential.'

That was no half-truth but a simple lie. He knew it, and the governor knew it too. The Great Cabin on *Sirius* had never offered solitude or quiet. At one end of the chart table, Rooke would be calculating the ship's longitude with the aid of Dr Vickery's *Almanac* and the *Requisite Tables*. At the other end, the midshipmen would be doing their navigation lessons. By the window the commodore would be at his own desk with his papers and charts. In the corner there might be an animated discussion between a couple of officers about, for instance, the respective merits from a culinary point of view of the various fish that the sailors were catching off the side. Rooke could be called on for his opinion and give it without missing a beat in his calculations.

The governor, isolated both by his position and, Rooke thought, his temperament, might have understood a man who enjoyed his own company best of all. But to allow him that enjoyment could look like an indulgence, and indulgence to one officer would open him to trouble from others.

The governor put his thumb under his chin and caressed his lip with a forefinger. Rooke could feel him performing a brief but complex calculation, one in which the need to demonstrate his authority against this mulish junior lieutenant was set against the future usefulness of a cooperative one. Rooke felt a flush of panic. Gilbert was nothing more than a naval captain of unremarkable talents, older but less gifted than himself. How was it that he could stand between a man and his proper life?

'Very well, Lieutenant Rooke. Have your headland. Let the Astronomer Royal get his comet. But, let me warn you, at the first sign of trouble you will be recalled. We are not so lavishly supplied with men. There may be a time when every musket is needed. And Lieutenant'—he lowered his voice—'speaking of that, I wish you to ensure that your weapon is loaded at all times.'

Then a private came bustling up and that was the end of the interview.

Out of sight of the governor Rooke stopped and laid a hand on his cheek, hot with the bitter flame of what he had so nearly lost.

Squeaked through, that was his thought. *A narrow squeak.* What squeaking? Why squeaking? It was a relief to wonder about the silly phrase rather than what would have happened if the governor had said *I regret, Lieutenant, but my decision is final, kindly do not ask again.*

He must remember how fragile his position was. There might be a destiny awaiting him here, but the governor was not interested in it. If he knew what was in his lieutenant's mind he would remind him that he was not a man of science, *an astronomer of the fairest promise,* but just another of the governor's subjects.

*

Unlike Greenwich, an antipodean observatory could not boast a majestic building with every convenience for an astronomer. The best approximation Rooke could devise was a small room surmounted by a cone of wood and canvas, something like an Indian teepee. The cone would have a long slit to accommodate the telescope, and its vertex would be a little off-centre to allow observations at the zenith.

It looked peculiar on his sketch, and he thought it would be peculiar when built. But there was a sharp pleasure in re-inventing the idea of an observatory from first principles.

Major Wyatt took the view that he could not be expected to pander to every whim—he did not spell out whether the whim was the lieutenant's or the governor's—but eventually he let Rooke have some men. They panted and scrambled up the ridge with the canvas and the poles for the tent that was to be Rooke's temporary home, with the bed and the table and the boxes of instruments.

Explaining his sketch to the carpenter, Rooke referred to the teepee as the dome. Perhaps dome was a little grand. He tried to explain why the cone had to be off-centre, went into detail about the need for the instruments to point straight up. He tried to use commonplace words, but he caught an astonished look in the man's eyes.

To speed the business along, Rooke laboured beside the others. A pick was awkward, he discovered, and his hand blistered from its rough wood. But, unlike the prisoners, he enjoyed his experience of heavy labour. Concentrating on striking the rock at just the right spot, and with just the right force, at just the right angle, he worked himself into a pleasantly mindless state.

The observation room was constructed on the top of the low cliff because of the solid base of rock it offered for the instruments. The hut for his own living quarters was below, connected to it by steps cut into the rock. Those steps—so simple to sketch—took the men twice as long as everything else put together. That was the difference between Euclid's world and the actual one.

What with rain, and the men being called away for other duties, it took months to get the thing finished. The awkward angles of timber and the puckered whitewashed canvas nailed to the dome gave the place an improvised look. The carpenter's pride was offended by the way the off-centre peak of the teepee looked as if he had made a mistake. The slit where the telescope would travel up and down showed its rough edges and the shutter that covered it was a crude thing of battens and canvas. He went away grumbling.

Rooke set his folding table on the floor of his living quarters and pushed his two chairs up to it. He arranged on the one and only shelf his razor, his pen and ink and his few books. He set up his stretcher in the corner, spread the blanket out, put on the pillow the Montaigne that had been Anne's farewell gift, and wedged the candle-holder into a crack in the wall for bedtime reading. In the dark corner behind the door he leaned his musket, the powder and shot hanging in their bags from a peg above it.

The carpenter had given him a window, or at least left a hole in the wall with a wooden shutter. Sitting at his table, Rooke looked out over the area of rock and tufts of grass that was now his front yard. Beyond that the land dropped away to the water, ruffled with the afternoon wind. A gull shot past with one powerful beat of its wings, down and up. Over on the opposite shore a wavering smudge of smoke rose above the trees.

The planks of the hut let in a cool winter wind, the shingles of the roof were already splitting. The fireplace stones were insufficiently stuck together with poor mortar and the floor bulged with elbows and knees of bedrock in spite of all Rooke's work with the pick. But nowhere on the world's surface had ever meant as much to him. It was his own, as no place had ever been other than the attic in Church Street, and it was private. If he wanted to converse with himself, he could. He had forgotten the pleasure of thinking aloud. There was no one here to judge, no one to remind him that being ordinary was hard work.

He felt as if he had been compressed, like a limb squeezed with a tourniquet, for all those years of school and shipboard life. Now, at last, he could expand to fill whatever space was proper to him. Out here, with his thoughts his only company, he could become nothing more or less than the person he was.

Himself. It was as unexplored a land as this one.

✳

Dr Vickery had predicted that his comet would return in the latter part of 1788, which was still some months distant. The comet would justify the existence of the astronomer, but in the meantime it was important to be seen as a conscientious man of science.

From their boxes Rooke got out the meteorological instruments that the Royal Observatory had provided: the thermometers from the Royal Society, the barometer, the anemometer, the specially constructed funnel and bottle for measuring rainfall. He was glad Dr Vickery could not see the instruments in their new setting. The Astronomer Royal would never need to know that the barometer and thermometer, the most advanced objects of their kind in Europe, hung from rope under the eaves of a hut as rough as a pig shed. He would never see the rain gauge sitting on the stump of a tree sawn off as level as could be managed, let alone know that the same stump performed the office of dressing table. It was a pleasure that Rooke would have to enjoy alone, that his life and his work were so little separate that, if he wished, he could conduct his researches whilst shaving.

All Dr Vickery would see were the ledgers in which the readings would be entered. They would represent a miracle of translation. The language of muddle, of wobble, of improvisation, would be transformed into exactitude. It was a shame, Rooke thought, that Dr Vickery could not share his delight in that transformation. *Winds, Weather, Barometer, Thermometer, Remarks.* Perhaps rashly, Rooke ruled up six observation times for every day, between four in the morning and eight at night. It was like the beginning of a grand enterprise to dip his pen in the ink and write up the first readings. *June 24, 1788. Wind: SSW, 4 knots. Weather: heavy cloud & hazy. Barometer: 29. Thermometer: 60.*

Remarks: About 7 h it began to rain and soon after the barometer rose.

Up the four lopsided steps from his living quarters, there was barely enough space in the observation room for one slender astronomer, and the canvas of the roof crackled distractingly in the wind. But the rock on which the quadrant stood had never been moved since the foundation of the world. Under his feet he could feel it, unmediated by floorboards or rug: the sphere of rock, spinning through space and time, taking himself and his instruments with it.

Through the telescope the stars burned with a foreign clarity, explosively brilliant, living things pulsing in the blackness. *For now we see through a glass, darkly; but then face to face.* He thought Paul must have been a man who had lain flat on his back on the ground and looked up at just such a sky as this.

Rooke knew the southern constellations now as well as those he had grown up with. All the way down the curve of the globe from Portsmouth to New South Wales he had watched them night by night creeping further up over the southern horizon. But at sea he had never seen them so bright.

The moon was crisp against the black sky, its seas and mountains as clear as if etched, upside down, of course, from the point of view of someone looking out the window of a parlour in misty Portsmouth.

He could have drawn that parlour, every crease in the table-cloth, every stain on the armchair, the place where the fringe of the rug was fraying. He could have told you how, at this moment—noon there, more or less, and summer of course—his father would be drawing his napkin out of his napkin ring and his mother would be slicing the bread and handing it to Anne to butter, and Bessie would be putting it on their plates, all of them suppressing the rumbling of their insides, impatient for the servant-girl to bring in the midday meal.

It was as real as that. He did not have to imagine the hunger, as the governor had them on short rations until the promised supply ships arrived from England. Yet it was also not real at all, a story someone had told him long ago about people in a dream.

From his stretcher he could hear the waters of the port, the restless sound coming in the window hole. The water was never still, always in conversation with itself and with the shore. He could hear it slapping up against the rocks at the foot of the point, knew how it must look, washing foamily into crannies. Nothing prevented a drop of that water from making in reverse the same voyage that he had. That drop could travel along the currents until it arrived at the Motherbank and slide past the Round Tower. It could splash up at last on the Hard, just where the tender from *Sirius* had pushed off with Daniel Rooke aboard a year before. It would leave a dark hieroglyph on one of the stones, a greeting from the far side of the globe to the world he had left behind.

Even after he took up residence in the observatory, Rooke joined the other officers for the Sunday dinner. He thought of it as a tithe of gratitude for not having to dine there on the other days.

One evening in the settlement's first winter, he arrived at the barracks—a long dark hut with an incongruously splendid mahogany table almost filling the space—to see the governor there at its head alongside Major Wyatt. It was an honour His Excellency paid now and again to his officers rather than dine alone in his own residence. Major Wyatt always thanked him fulsomely. As far as the rest of them were concerned, the governor's presence made for careful conversation.

Rooke installed himself between Silk and young Lieutenant Timpson and, he hoped, out of the line of sight of Major Wyatt and the governor. Timpson was tedious, inveighing against the women prisoners—all damned whores in his view—and forever bringing out the miniature of his sweetheart, expecting wonderment and admiration from other men. He was too young and artless to know that another man's sweetheart in an oval frame was of limited interest.

Silk's opinion of young Lieutenant Timpson was that he protested too much. *Mark my words, Rooke*, Silk had said. *We will be seeing him with us at Mrs Butcher's before the end of the year and will hear no more of this Betsy.* Rooke was inclined to agree. Mrs Butcher had kept an establishment in Devizes, apparently, and knew how to run a good house. Sometimes with Silk and sometimes alone, Rooke had visited her hut and found her to be both hospitable and discreet, offering the choice of several pleasant convict girls and the privacy of a canvas curtain.

Timpson's innocent prudery was tedious, but Rooke was happy to admire Betsy for the hundredth time, and agree what a sweet and dear face she had, if it allowed him to take his place in the furthest and most dimly lit corner of the room.

At the head of the table, the governor and Wyatt sat glumly as the boy set their plates of food in front of them. Silk broke the silence.

'Ah, the daily diabolical morsel!'

It was a risk, Rooke thought, to draw attention to what was on each plate, but the governor went so far as to laugh. Wyatt followed, and the whole table joined in. Only Silk could have got away with it, but he had judged well: men confronted with yet another insufficient meal of elderly salt beef and a spoonful of pease porridge were glad of any distraction.

His Majesty's victualler had assumed that New South Wales would produce at least some of the food its colonists needed, but this had proved to be optimistic. The heart of the mop-like tree was called cabbage, although Rooke thought it as fibrous and probably as tasty as oakum. Various sparse greens grew by the stream, and the leaves of a sprawling vine had been found to make a faintly sweet tea which he had come to savour. That was the extent of the vegetable production of the place.

Gardens had been planted, but what with the grubs, soil that was no better than sand, and theft by prisoners, no turnip or potato had ever grown bigger than a marble.

Now and then the governor's shooter brought back game from the woods. His Excellency was generous in sharing it with his officers, and Rooke, like the others, had relished the various unrecognisable joints of tough but tasty meat. No part of the creatures was wasted, since Surgeon Weymark paid the shooter for the heads. Rooke had seen Weymark's watercolours, the stump where the kangaroo or opossum neck had been hacked off with the hatchet cunningly hidden in the picture by a spray of foliage.

But the fact remained: supplies were running short.

The mess cook spread the food out as he served it, to make it look more substantial. To Rooke, the stratagem suggested an interesting calculation: how large a circle could be made with a given quantity of pease and salt beef?

But whether thin or thick, whatever diameter its circle, and no matter how interesting the problem involving pi, the food was insufficient, because the supply ships were nowhere to be seen.

'Those buggers have forgotten us,' Timpson said *sotto voce* to Rooke, running a finger around his plate and sucking at it. 'Spat us out and said good riddance. Or else the ships are all wrecked. I wish to God I had not volunteered.'

It was Timpson's first appointment and he had not yet learned to hide his homesickness. As he ate he was inclined to dream aloud of his favourite meals, especially his mother's hotpot with braised leeks. Rooke too had caught himself daydreaming about a dish of new potatoes with butter and parsley and salt, and a nice fresh mutton chop to go with it.

Around the table, on which every plate soon gleamed, Rooke thought there was not a single man who believed that His Majesty's newest settlement would last. It was only a matter of whether they all starved first.

At the end of the meal the governor rose in his place, looking so spindly and angular that Rooke was put in mind of Newton's Mathematical Bridge.

'Good evening, gentlemen, and my thanks for your hospitality.'

He glanced down at his plate and hesitated as if regretting

the ironic possibilities of the remark.

'It is my intention to take a party of men into the hinter-land. I hope to locate whatever it might offer that could be turned to account.'

Turned to account. They all knew the fact behind that fine turn of phrase: *Nothing will grow at Sydney Cove and our store is running out.*

'I am confident also that we will fall in with natives more prepared to parley with us than those we have encountered here.'

Rooke thought of those two men who had walked past him as if he were a rock or a bush. Every day his first act was to go outside and see if they had returned.

The governor stretched his face into his approximation of a smile.

'I wonder whether any of you gentlemen would care to be of the party.'

Rooke did not stop to think, jumped to his feet.

'Lieutenant Rooke sir, I will go.'

Birds—mammals—ants and their habitations. This was his chance to see more of New South Wales than the speck of it he was so far familiar with. And if there should be an opportunity to parley, who better to do it than a man who knew five languages?

Silk was only a little behind.

'Captain Silk also, sir, at your service,' he called out.

At your service, that was a better form of words. Rooke tucked it away. Less like a schoolboy than *I will go!* He felt himself blushing, but no one was watching.

'Thank you, gentlemen, I am obliged to you.'

After the meal Silk hung back.

'My word, Rooke, I thought myself the quickest jack-in-the-box in the regiment, but I see I must not be complacent!'

Rooke tried to frame a reply, but Silk did not wait.

'Prickles, sunburn, mosquitoes, and, I doubt not, snakes. Perhaps unfriendly natives too. However, the worse it is to experience, the better it will read on the page. The natives are what I need. Their shyness is disappointing. This expedition may provide an opportunity to chat to the elusive fellows. And whatever other outcomes, we will have brought a little favourable attention on ourselves.'

He winked.

'The long view, my friend, never lose sight of the long view of our time in New South Wales.'

The long view was hard to keep sight of when faced with New South Wales one yard at a time. Rooke sat in the cutter with the rest of the party, hearing the dip and suck of the oars as the sailors propelled them along the harbour towards the west. In the bow, the governor had a thwart to himself, peering with his telescope. Silk sat alertly behind him, now and then leaning forward to respond to some remark from the governor that Rooke could not hear. Beside Silk, Lieutenant Willstead also leaned forward, his bony face eager, trying to make his mark. Willstead had been on *Sirius*. All the way across the Atlantic, all the way across the Great Southern Ocean, Rooke had watched him trying in vain to make his mark with the governor. His ambition was too naked on his lean face, his ingratiating smile too much a matter of mechanics. Silk had just as much ambition, but did not seem to care, and when the governor turned on his thwart to comment on some point of interest, it was always to Silk that he spoke.

Behind Rooke sat two privates on either side of a big bearded prisoner: the governor's shooter, Silk had told Rooke, brought along to bag them their suppers. He was like a haunch of beef himself, Rooke thought, his massive shoulders all of a piece with his powerful neck. He met the man's eyes: shrewd, knowing, sceptical.

Lieutenant Gardiner of *Sirius* was in charge of the boat. He balanced himself in the stern while the sailors laboured over the oars, steering them up the harbour. On the northern shore, high dark prows of headlands hung over the water, the sombre woods pressing down into their own reflections. To the south the land was lower, each bay and promontory shining with the glossy leaves of mangroves. Now and then between them a crescent of yellow sand was like a punctuation mark. Gulls bobbing on the water turned their heads to watch the boat pass, pelicans seemed to smile to themselves. The tide was behind the boat, sweeping it around bend after bend, the banks narrowing until what had been a harbour became a river.

They rounded a long low promontory and found themselves sliding past a slope of grass on which four or five natives sat around a fire, staring at the boat. They were like a tableau being dragged across a stage. And of course, from the point of view of the natives, the boatful of staring strangers must be a tableau sliding through their field of view.

'Turn in, Lieutenant,' the governor called along the boat to Gardiner. 'Back oars and bring us in to them.'

He stood up in the bow as the boat drew closer, took off his hat and waved it.

'Good morning!' he shouted. 'Good morning, friends!'

The natives did not wave back. As Rooke watched, the tableau moved and a woman rose from beside the fire, scooping up a child against her breast, and walked away into the bushes. One by one the others got up and followed her. They did not seem to be hurrying but, by the time the boat was close enough to land, the clearing was empty.

'Shall I jump ashore, sir?' Willstead asked. 'I could jump ashore, sir, and go after them.'

But there was something about Willstead's voice that the governor could not seem to hear.

'Row on, Lieutenant Gardiner,' he called, an edge in his voice. 'We will not waste time here.'

The river narrowed to a stream winding between deep banks and finally their way was blocked by flat slabs of rock piled up in shelves down which water tinkled and shone.

'Terminus, gentlemen!' Gardiner called, and backed the boat in to where one of the slabs of rock fell away into deep water.

Willstead and Silk got out and turned to help the governor,

but he was getting his angles and joints out over the gunwale with considerable dexterity.

'Thank you, gentlemen, but as you see, I am already here.'

He looked up at the steep banks on either side, scoured to bare rock in places by past floods, and was already setting off while he gave orders over his shoulder.

'Thank you, Lieutenant Gardiner, I will expect you at this spot in three days' time. Now Captain Silk, come alongside me if you please, we will lead the way. Lieutenant Willstead, will you be good enough to come after us. Lieutenant Rooke, be so kind as to bring up the rear and record our line of march. Sergeant, you and the privates will march with the gamekeeper.'

Rooke laughed, thinking the governor had made one of his rare witticisms, but he turned in his angled way and fixed him with a cold eye. Rooke coughed into his hand.

Gamekeeper! The word suggested the society that Lancelot Percival James had boasted of at the Academy: pheasants and deer in a park artfully planted to enhance the prospect, cheerful peasantry tipping their caps to the squire riding by.

But New South Wales was no gentleman's estate. His Majesty's subjects were perched in a small sour clearing on the edge of the unknown. The land around them seemed without resources either animal or vegetable, and the gamekeeper was a criminal who had been given a gun.

The party fell in behind the governor. From the rear, Rooke

could see the line of knapsacks bobbing along, and the heads bowed to avoid the whippy bushes. The prisoner, taller than anyone else, his powerful frame half bursting out of its threadbare check shirt, shouldered through everything in his path. He carried the governor's knapsack as well as his own, but they sat on his back like baubles.

The governor's announced aim had been to strike due west, but the party needed constantly to diverge north or south to avoid muddy creeks too wide to cross and impenetrable thickets where shrubs had engulfed fallen trees. They climbed down ravines full of creepers that caught around their ankles and hauled themselves up the steep rocky slopes on the other side from which they could see only another ravine.

At the back of the line, Rooke had a compass in one hand, a notebook in the other, his pencil behind his ear, counting his paces and noting each change of direction. He had ruled up the pages beforehand: *Number of paces. Direction of march.* As he scrawled in the columns he decided that the words *march* and *direction* did not do justice to the reality.

The place flowed past, a blur of namelessness. *Tree. Another tree. Bush. Another sort of bush. White flower. Yellow flower. Red flower.* To be unable to give things their proper names was to be like a child again. He remembered himself on the shingle below the Round Tower, crouching over his pebble collection: *big one, small one, light one, dark one.*

The governor called a halt for the night beside a stream

fringed with tall reeds. Rooke sat down and peeled off the knapsack, stuck to his back with sweat that was cooling unpleasantly as the evening chill came over the woods.

He watched as the sergeant reluctantly gave the prisoner a gun and a bag of shot. The man took the musket—like a toy in his enormous hand—and hefted the bag of shot in a practised way. He smiled from behind his beard, his lips rosy.

'You want supper, sir, it will want to be a damned sight more shot than that!' he said.

'Mind your tongue, man,' the sergeant was beginning, but the governor called out, 'It is all right, Sergeant, Brugden is to have whatever he needs.'

The sergeant's mouth became a compressed line as he doled out another handful of shot. Brugden grinned, showing powerful white teeth.

'Thank you, Sergeant,' he said. 'Thank you so very much indeed, sir.'

The sergeant watched him go, swaggering along the creek, the gun over his shoulder, his shadow long on the grass. On the hulks, Rooke thought, the man would not have been allowed even a pocketknife for cutting his bread. The sour-faced sergeant looked as though he were thinking the same thing.

The governor saw Rooke watching the man stride off.

'When in Rome, Mr Rooke,' he said. 'I know Brugden from home, he was a gamekeeper for the Duke of Portland before he unfortunately fell foul of the law, he is a rough sort of fellow but

I have seen him hit a woodpigeon at a hundred paces.'

'But sir, if he wanders?' Willstead suggested.

The governor gave him a wry look. 'Yes, Lieutenant Willstead, if he wanders? Can you tell me where you think he might get to?'

Willstead blinked but had no answer.

Rooke sat down on a log and got out his notebook to tot up the paces and compass bearings. Thinking he might find it useful in the wilderness, he had paced out along Church Street, Portsmouth, Anne running beside him with the chalk, marking each step. The average length of stride of Lieutenant Daniel Rooke was thirty-three inches.

Here, stumbling, climbing and creeping by turns, such precision was irrelevant. Like Euclid, he would begin with an assertion and, since he was inventing, he might as well make the arithmetic simple: *Let each pace be thirty-six inches.*

When he had tallied everything up he marked their line of march on the sketch map of the place. It was a strange zigzag like the path of a beetle rather than a detachment of the king's armed forces.

He got up to take it to the governor but Silk intercepted him.

'How many miles, Rooke? How far to the west?'

Rooke pointed at where his zigzag line ended.

'By my reckoning, we are four and five-eighths miles south-west of the place we disembarked,' he said.

'Four and five-eighths? My word, you are a marvel, Lieutenant!'

Silk turned to Willstead, who had his shoes and spatter-dashes off and was sitting on a fallen log touching delicately at his blisters.

'Look, Willstead, can you believe it, Rooke can put us exactly here.'

Silk placed his finger with finicking exactness on the spot where the dotted line ended.

Willstead barely looked at the paper.

'My word,' he said. 'Well done, Rooke.'

He did not try to conceal that his blisters were of more interest to him than a mark on a sheet of paper. Silk watched him, his mouth rather set, his chin somewhat drawn in. It was the look he had when Rooke answered a question too exhaus-tively. *Exasperation* was the word to describe it, Rooke thought, though Silk was too genial and too gentlemanly to do more than this hardly visible tightening of a few muscles.

'Thank you, Rooke,' he said warmly, as if making up for Willstead's indifference. 'I find it steadying to be able to locate myself so precisely.'

He glanced around at the bushes pressing down the slope towards them so that Rooke wondered whether it was really praise or a subtle mockery.

Leaving the others he paced along the bank of the stream with the compass in his hand. *Establishing the course of the tributary,* he explained to some imaginary questioner. *Taking advantage of the last of the light.* When he pushed aside a bush to get down to the water, a duck burst up from under his feet. He leaped back in fright. It fluttered along and skidded onto the water quacking with a sound like laughter. *Heck heck heck! Heck heck!*

A place so strange took a layer of skin off a man and left him peeled.

He made a show of noting the way the stream hooked to the north, but the reality was that he wanted simply to be able to see what was around him. Unrelenting newness made for something like blindness. It was as if sight did not function properly in the absence of understanding. Without his pack and his notebook, he hoped that his eyes might begin to make distinctions among all those trees and bushes.

The grass by the stream was tender in the thickening dusk, sucking up the horizontal rays of the sun and turning a green so bright it seemed liquid. Beside the stream the fir trees drooped. *Firs:* it was what everyone called them. But when he pulled off a spray of the needles he saw that, unlike a fir's, they were jointed, the knuckles packed together more closely at the tip. What leaf grew like a telescope, pushing itself out segment by segment?

He had wanted strangeness. Well, this place was strange beyond comprehension.

The gamekeeper came back just before dark with a brace of parrots and an opossum. His time in the woods had energised him.

'Not much by way of game, sir,' Rooke heard him telling the governor. 'But if it moves, sir, well then I shoot it!'

Brugden was flushed with satisfaction, watching with pride as one of the privates dealt with feathers and fur. The creatures made a stew of sorts that was hardly enticing, but helped the small ration of hard old bread along.

After the meal Rooke, like everyone else, was glad to roll himself into his blanket. His thighs quivered from the day of remorseless up and down, he had been bitten by a thousand insects and the blanket was insufficient against the cold of the night.

But, as sleep descended, the thought came to him: *There is nowhere in the world that I would rather be.*

∗

They had left the river behind on their journey west, but on the second day they found it again. Along the bank a path had been worn by feet before theirs.

'Ah,' the governor exclaimed. 'At last we may meet some natives!'

Rooke wondered how an exchange might begin. By going forward and offering words, he supposed. That first day on the beach, he should have tried fewer trinkets and more words. He had missed another opportunity the day those two men had passed his hut.

He would not miss a third chance. He rehearsed it: the laying down of the musket, the stepping towards them with empty hands outstretched. He would not wait for the governor, he would take the initiative. But then? How would the dialogue start?

No natives appeared to put the question to the test, but a hundred and thirty-four paces later they saw trees bleeding red sap from fresh scars. Two hundred and seven paces further brought them to a cluster of native huts and a smouldering fire.

'They cannot be far away,' Willstead said.

'That is perfectly true, Lieutenant,' the governor replied. 'What a shame it is that we do not know in which direction.'

The bushes and trees around them could have hidden an army.

'Where are they?' the governor demanded irritably. 'Why do they hide from us?'

Willstead took it on himself to answer.

'I imagine, sir, that they are waiting to see how we declare ourselves. When they understand our peaceable intentions they will approach.'

But the governor was too exasperated to want soft soap.

'But when, Mr Willstead? When might they condescend to speak with us?'

The river widened and the land on either side curved upwards more gently, the undergrowth gone, the trees standing apart from each other among grass. Here, as nowhere else, the idea of a gentleman's park was not altogether ridiculous.

The governor called a halt.

'Captain Silk, the trowel if you please.'

He dug up a handful of dark dirt and made a fist around it, inspecting the crumbling ball he produced. He peered, he sniffed. Was he going to taste it? Silk, standing solemnly by with the trowel, caught Rooke's eye with a droll expression.

'Lieutenant Rooke,' the governor said, turning so that Silk had to re-arrange his face, 'would you be so good as to note the location of this spot, it is my view that this soil would reward cultivation.'

Rooke got out his notebook and compass, took bearings from a nearby hill, drew a line representing the river, and generally made a big work of establishing where they were.

'I am obliged to you, Lieutenant,' the governor said, and favoured him with one of his squeezed smiles.

*

That evening Brugden was again given the gun and shot and boasted that this time he would bring back something better than opossum.

'Put your minds at rest, gentlemen,' he announced to Rooke and Willstead as he set off. 'If there is anything worth eating out there, I promise you it will not get away. If it moves, well then by God I shoot it!'

He swaggered off with the gun over his shoulder.

'My mind was not especially agitated, in point of fact,' Willstead muttered to Rooke. 'That fellow has been given too much latitude, in my view.'

He watched Brugden go with a sourness he did not try to hide.

Half an hour later as they sat by the fire they heard the retort of a distant gun.

'Dinner, I imagine,' Silk said.

But a short time later there was a tremendous crashing down the hillside and Brugden burst out of the bushes, cap falling over one ear, his beard full of leaves, and a humid swollen look to one eye.

'The buggers stoned me,' he bellowed, 'saving your presence, sir, but the damned buggers stoned me.'

He held out an arm, showing a swollen red graze.

The governor was not interested in the man's arm.

'What happened, Brugden,' he snapped. 'Quick to it now and tell me straight.'

At this Rooke thought the prisoner looked a little shifty. He struck Rooke as a man with a sharp assessment of where his own interests lay.

'I never did nothing, sir,' he said. 'I were just walking along, I had got a couple of crows, I were just taking a bead on one of them opossums, then I get a stone smack in the back, another on the arm here, the bushes was that thick I couldn't see nothing, sir, not one thing!'

Like Rooke, the governor seemed to hear too much protest in this.

'And then? Did you shoot? Out with it, man!'

Brugden's beard made it easy for him to hide the expression on his face.

'They was coming for me, they had the spears and the cudgels, I felt my life to be in danger, sir.'

'So you did see them! Did you shoot?'

Brugden avoided his gaze, rubbing at the place on his arm and another place on his neck. His eye was almost closed.

'Yes, sir,' he said truculently. 'I fired among the thick of them, sir, if not, sir, I'd be a dead man.'

The governor looked at the ground as if tamping down rage.

'So you fired. Did you wound? Did any fall?'

'Why, sir, I fired and then I run. I could not say what happened, I let off the gun then I ran like the blazes, I had the fear of God in me, sir.'

'Brugden, I warned you, if you remember.'

The governor's voice was so soft that Rooke had to lean in to hear.

'I warned you, I told you, and now I will tell you once again. The survival of this settlement, and of all its members, depends in large degree on maintaining cordial relations with the natives.

Do you understand, man? There are too few of us, and God knows how many of them.'

'Yes, sir,' Brugden said.

His rosy lips shaped the words like a small creature in the thicket of dark hair, then disappeared.

The mood of the party shifted with Brugden's story. Rooke saw the governor have a word with Silk, saw Silk have a word with the sergeant, saw one of the privates take up position as guard. The sergeant discreetly gathered up the guns and loaded them in the shadows beyond the fire, then brought them back and laid them in a row.

Rooke supposed he should be frightened. In their different ways, he thought the others were. Brugden was surly, groaning each time he moved, squinting through his closed-up eye. Willstead got his stockings and shoes back on and sat on a log by the fire repeatedly clearing his throat like a man about to give his wedding speech. Silk slapped at the mosquitoes with larger gestures than necessary.

'My God they are the size of sparrows, I swear, even though you would think them discouraged by the cold,' he exclaimed. 'Rooke, I have no doubt you hoped for natural curiosities unknown to science, but frankly, my friend, wondrous though you no doubt find them, I would as soon forgo the pleasure of their acquaintance.'

It was theatre, Rooke thought, the lit-up clearing by the fire a stage on which a performance was taking place, entitled perhaps *His Majesty's Men Defy the Foe.*

He chewed through his ration, making it last. Even crow soup would have been welcome. Something had happened out there in the woods about which Brugden was remaining silent. But if native warriors were planning to attack, a few muskets were not going to save them. Fear was what you felt when your actions could make a difference to what was about to happen. Eight men alone in this immensity of unknown could only wait and hope.

It was an uneasy night, but an uneventful one. They woke to long calm stripes of sunlight along the grass between the trees, and the carolling of birds welcoming the day. In sunlight, the row of loaded muskets seemed absurd.

That day they closed off the ragged three-quarter circle they had described and made their way back to where they had disembarked. As they glimpsed the boat through the trees the governor turned to Rooke.

'First-rate navigating, Lieutenant Rooke. Well done.'

Gardiner had the boat neatly backed in to the shore. Rooke watched him read the governor's face and see that the promised land of sweet pasture and talkative natives had not been found. He gave Rooke a private grimace that said, *Rather you than me.*

Rooke was pleased to be sitting in the boat taking his ease rather than stumbling along with his pack. But he had established himself as a *first-rate navigator.* That would not do him any harm at all. And that long blundering through a nameless land was like the first meeting with a stranger: a promise of something better to come.

Silk had his pencil out and was jotting something down in his notebook and smiling at the words. Willstead had managed to get himself beside the governor but when the governor spoke, it was Silk he turned around to address.

'That fertile area by the river is exactly what I hoped we might find,' Rooke heard him say. 'It looks fair to become the breadbasket of the colony, would you not say, Captain Silk?'

'Indeed, sir,' Silk said. 'Very promising, a fair prospect indeed.'

He met Rooke's glance but, with the governor next to him, even Silk did not dare wink.

Brugden's eye was a regal shade of purple, and he had gone silent and grim. It was more than the pain, Rooke thought. The man had been humiliated, and would not forget it.

U nusually, the governor was also at the next Sunday
dinner at the barracks. As the officers took their
places, he was already standing, leaning forward with
his fingertips on the mahogany, barely containing his impatience.

'Gentlemen,' he started, before everyone was quite seated.
'Gentlemen!'

Major Wyatt struck his fork against his wine glass and glared
down the table at where Gosden was coughing.

'I have to announce a highly important discovery, made on
our recent expedition,' the governor announced. 'It is of a most
excellently promising place for agriculture. The soil is of a
surpassing fertility and well watered by a noble river. I have
named the place Rose Hill.'

Rose Hill, Rooke thought, that untamed place where no rose had ever grown? Where the soil was fertile only by comparison with the grey sand of Sydney Cove?

'I have the intention of establishing a second settlement there, guarded by a small garrison. Captain Lennox has done me the honour of accepting the task.'

Everyone looked along the table to Lennox, who got to his feet, bowed his long bony body, and sat again. Rooke observed that he did not allow his spine to touch the back of the chair. Even sitting, Lennox was at attention.

'Captain Lennox is to take a party of men and prisoners there as soon as practicable. Agriculture will be initiated at the earliest opportunity. I have every confidence that the place will rapidly feed our infant colony.'

Lennox blinked once, his face inscrutable. Around the table only Silk moved. One hand went to his hair and smoothed it back from his brow. His eyes found Rooke's and his face moved in a flicker that no one could accuse of being a wink.

Confidence was one word for the governor's enthusiasm, Rooke thought. Another might be *delusion.* But the governor was paid to be optimistic. His fifteen hundred pounds a year would cease if the settlement were abandoned. Fifteen hundred pounds bought a great deal of confidence.

The governor held up his empty plate.

'After that time, gentlemen, I can promise there will be no more of these!'

Wyatt demonstrated that the governor had made a joke by forcing a loud laugh. A few others joined in. Wyatt missed nothing, so Rooke quirked up the corners of his mouth in what he thought was probably a smirk, but even the worst smile was better than none.

The governor looked pleased at the reception of his pleasantry. He had grown paler and more brittle with every week that passed. Everyone knew that he was on meagre rations too, had even donated his private stock of flour into the common store.

'In the short term, in order to supplement the diabolical morsel'—he bowed towards Silk—'I have decided to appoint two more prisoners to join Brugden as gamekeepers. Brugden is confident that they will be able to supply fresh meat on a regular basis and in considerable quantity.'

Rooke thought of Brugden, out there in the woods, that powerful chest, the gun as easy on his shoulder as if part of his body. He would be an efficient killer. Rooke imagined the woods like a body of water, in which the ripples of Brugden's destruction would go out and out, wider and wider. With three men on the job, the place would soon be stripped of game.

'On the matter of the natives,' the governor went on, 'it is a source of regret that they have proved so reluctant to come among us. I have every confidence that, if they were to do so, they would discover that we have nothing but good will towards them. The obstacle has, of course, been the lack of opportunity to demonstrate such good will. I am, however, confident'— Rooke saw him hesitate, as if hearing his repetition of the word—'that this situation may shortly be rectified.'

Rooke felt for the man, watching him cling so fiercely to optimism. With every tree cut down, every yard of ground dug and planted, his need became more urgent: to convey to the natives that new masters of the soil had come upon their demesne. In the absence of any understanding about the new arrangements, Rooke could see that there was a dangerous ambiguity to the presence of a thousand of His Majesty's subjects in this place. No such understanding was possible without language to convey it, and persons to whom the news could be delivered. And yet it seemed that the silence might continue indefinitely.

The governor would not have welcomed warfare, but Rooke thought he would have understood it. War was a species of conversation. But this silence was neither war nor peace. It was a null that paralysed the small frail figure straining to stand straight in front of his officers.

✳

The pleasure of precision was one unsung by poets, as far as he knew, but for Rooke the small thrill of marking the afternoon readings of the instruments into the prepared spot in his ledger never failed. *September 14, 1788 4 pm. Wind: NE, 8 knots.* If he were ever to attempt a poem, he thought he would take exactitude as his subject.

But how would he make rhymes out of the words he would have to use? Perhaps that was why there were no odes to the thermometer or the rain gauge.

Thinking about Silk, who could probably suggest such rhymes, there was an instant's confusion in his mind as he saw that the man coming down the rocks towards him was not Silk, but Gardiner.

Rooke got up to welcome him. Gardiner would have even less idea than he did himself of how one might find a rhyme for thermometer, but the idea would entertain him.

Usually hearty, Gardiner greeted Rooke in a preoccupied way, sat at the table and downed in one swig his brandy-and-water.

Gardiner could be an odd sort of fellow. As another odd sort of fellow, Rooke knew how to be patient.

When Gardiner spoke, his voice cracked so he had to cough and start again.

'It was not well done, Rooke,' he said. 'It was a shocking bad thing to do.'

'What is it, old fellow, tell me?' Rooke asked, to give Gardiner a little momentum. 'I hear nothing out here. In my eyrie. You will have to tell me.'

Gardiner took a breath like a sigh.

'You know the governor is wanting to speak to the natives, and they will not come near. He came up with a way to settle the thing. Decided in his wisdom to seize one or two by force. Teach them English, learn their tongue. Treat them well, so they would tell the others. It was me he picked to do the dirty work.'

He was silent for so long that Rooke thought he might say no more.

'He was most particular,' Gardiner said at last. 'We were to take the cutter down to the cove inside North Head, someone had seen a party of natives there. We were to take some fish with us, lure a couple of the men away. You know how they love fish.'

He wiped a hand over his face.

'We got ourselves backed into the shallow water there, held up the fish. Well, they were smart enough to be careful at the start. But we called and coaxed and dangled the damned fish… we grabbed two poor devils, they were slippery as eels and fought like the blazes but I had eight good men there, we got the ropes around them in the end.'

Rooke could see it: the boat lurching, the native men sprawled in the water slopping about in the bottom, pinned there with the sheer poundage of cursing sailors. He wanted to hear the next part of the tale, in which the natives threw off the sailors, leaped out of the boat, swam ashore, vanished into the woods.

'I cannot believe that the governor,' he started, but Gardiner was not listening.

'They cried out, Rooke,' Gardiner exclaimed. 'By God you should have heard them crying out, it would break your heart. The ones left behind as we got away, they were screaming. The wretches in the boat crying out. Oh God. They may be savages, we call them savages. But their feelings are no different from ours.'

He jumped up as if the chair had grown spikes and went over to the window. Rooke could see only his big shoulders, the back of his head. The hut was silent. Even the water at the foot of the rocks was holding its breath.

Rooke half rose out of his chair, not knowing what to do next, only that he could not let Gardiner stand there alone. But as he moved, Gardiner took a long shaky breath that ended in a cough, dragged out his handkerchief and blew his nose. He came back to the table and poured himself a drink, his hands shaking.

'Well, they are in the hut behind the governor's house now. He had the shackles put on them, I am glad I did not have to watch that.'

'You did your duty, that was all.'

How feeble that sounded. What did duty have to do with a man undone by feeling?

'You did it in the kindliest way. That such a task could be done. Since it had to be done.'

'Kindly!' Gardiner repeated. 'He will put it in that light, you may be sure of it. In London they will all agree. How kindly.

What a splendid fellow, best give him another fifty pound a year.'

Rooke knew Gardiner as well as he knew any man, but had never dreamed that he might speak with this depth of bitterness. Or how some answering sharpness in himself was responding. He had not known how much he had come to dislike the governor, that secretive sour man.

'*Brought in*, that is what he calls it. The natives were *brought in*. Never mind that they were kidnapped. Violently. Against their will. They were crying, Rooke, I tried to show them we meant no harm, but they were wailing as if their hearts would break! Who will say how it really was? Tell the truth about it?'

'Certainly not a pair of lieutenants who know which side their bread is buttered!' It was an effort to lighten the mood, but Rooke might as well not have spoken.

'It was by far the most unpleasant service I ever was ordered to execute.'

Gardiner's voice was low, ashamed. Rooke thought, *And I? Have I ever been given an order that would shake me, shame me?* Nothing came to his mind. On *Resolution* he could not see the men his blind shots might have reached, if there had been any. In New South Wales he had sidestepped the whole business of being a soldier through the good offices of astronomy. But it was chance, nothing more. There was a coldness in him, knowing that only accident lay between his situation and Gardiner's.

A loose shingle rattled, the branch of a bush scratched

against the wall. A bird warbled once, twice.

'I wish to God I had not done it! He should not have given the order, but I wish to God I had not obeyed!'

Gardiner was shouting, the words filling the hut and sailing out the window.

'For God's sake, man! Have a care what you say!'

They were private out here, but no degree of privacy was safe when such words were released into the air. The lieutenant who had twirled at the end of the rope that day in English Harbour had not got as far as disobeying. Nor had the other two, the ones Rooke had watched being sent into oblivion. The words had been enough. Here, where all that stood between the governor and chaos was a handful of officers, no hint of insubordination could be tolerated.

'Our duty,' he began, 'our duty as soldiers,' but his friend had already drawn back. Gardiner drank off his cupful and screwed a grin onto his face that stretched his sunburnt sailor's lips.

'Yes, Mr Rooke, I know. Yes, we are all servants of the governor here and the Devil take any man who says different!'

Rooke said nothing more. There was a question forming in the back of his mind, which he did not want to hear. It was: *What would I have done in the same place?*

＊

Early next morning Rooke went down to the settlement. He felt disloyal to Gardiner, but he was consumed with curiosity about the captured natives. He wondered by what stratagem he might get a glimpse of them, but none was necessary. As he passed the parade ground he saw the governor walking down the hill with two men shuffling in fetters. Captain Silk was looking sprightly at the governor's elbow, a notebook and pencil in his hand.

The bigger of the natives was a finely made man, perhaps thirty years old. There was a roguish sparkle to his eye. It made Rooke think that if Silk were to have been kidnapped, and became the guest of some unimaginable chief of the natives, he would look around in just that way, with eyes that found everything interesting, and the smile of someone having the greatest adventure of his life.

The other was a person of different make, shorter and sterner, a compact mass of outraged dignity. Being here was not an adventure for him, Rooke thought. It was an affront to his sense of himself.

The governor's narrow face had changed overnight, broadening and beaming. Today he was not nearly so much like the Mathematical Bridge. He held up his hand to the cheerful captive and turned it.

'Now, Boinbar. This is what we call "hand". What is the word in your tongue?'

Bo-in-bar. Rooke saw it as if written, committed it to memory. His first word of the native tongue.

Silk licked the end of his pencil and made ready to write the native word for 'hand'. *The quickest jack-in-the-box in the regiment.* How had Silk got himself there with the notebook in his hand, Rooke wondered. If one wanted a linguist in New South Wales, would one not ask for Lieutenant Rooke?

Perhaps the governor enjoyed the company of an officer of his own size, he thought, and was shocked at himself. *There will be time,* he told himself. *Silk is no linguist, and then they will remember me.*

Now the governor was trying to gain the attention of the other man, holding up his thumb and waggling it.

'Warungin? Warungin! Here is my thumb, we say "thumb", now tell me what you say.'

Wa-rung-in. Two words of the native tongue.

But Warungin would not meet the governor's eye and had no interest in his thumb. Even though hobbled by the fetters he walked upright and stared into the middle distance as though the governor were not there.

These men were like, but not like, those Rooke had seen in Antigua. They were not as tall as the slaves and their skin was not that black that was almost blue. Theirs was a warmer, browner black. Nor did they have those swollen lips, fascinating in their fullness, that the Africans had.

As well as those differences they were born with, there were others that he thought life might teach. These two men of New South Wales carried themselves proudly erect, yielding to no one. Isolation had saved them from becoming like those uprooted Africans he had seen in English Harbour, expression-less black cogs in the machine of empire.

Boinbar looked straight at Rooke, at the red wool coat, the brass buttons, the gold braid, at the straight hair, the smooth cheeks, the pale skin. Under his gaze Rooke saw how strange it might be to have such hair, such skin. To cover the body with fabric and small shiny objects.

His eyes met Boinbar's and he felt a bubble of laughter in his throat. He saw his own excitement reflected on the other man's face, the same eagerness to enter the unknown, to be amazed by difference.

But now the governor was turning back towards his house,

putting a hand under Boinbar's elbow.

'Come, my friend, we will eat now.'

He made large champing motions and hand-to-mouth actions, and Boinbar went with him willingly enough. Silk had to urge Warungin to follow, going so far as to touch his arm, but Warungin withdrew it. Shuffling in the fetters, his face rock-like, he walked up the road, a muscular nugget of disapproval.

*

Several times in the two weeks following, Rooke found reasons to go down to the settlement, hoping to see more of the native men, but they were never about. Young Timpson told him they spent most of their time at the governor's house, being shown how to sit on a chair and eat off a plate. But poor homesick Timpson was not much interested in anything that was not about his Betsy, and he had no other information.

Rooke had wanted solitude, had schemed to be cut off from the settlement. He had congratulated himself on achieving it. But, like Midas, he had his riches and was the poorer for them. His isolation was robbing him of the chance to stand beside Silk and exchange words with the native men.

He put his mind to some pretext for calling at the governor's house. The ledger was all he could think of. He might request a meeting with the governor and pretend to ask his advice about any improvements that His Excellency might suggest, before he filled in too many of its pages. Should he, for example, be recording the height of the tides as well as the wind and weather?

It was a shallow ruse, but who knew how long it would be before he could see more of those new planets Boinbar and Warungin?

He was transcribing his most recent readings into their columns, planning to take the ledger down the next day, when he heard someone hallooing outside: Captain Silk, picking his way down between the rocks.

'Rooke,' he called. 'A visitor to your enchanted isle!'

Silk jumped athletically down the last few yards, lost his balance, nearly tripped, did a quick to-and-fro with his feet and had arrived.

'By God, you are secret out here,' he cried, suppressing his panting. 'A man needs to be a goat to pay you a visit!'

Sure of his welcome, he did not wait for an answer, but went inside.

'Well, my friend, will you not offer me something cheerful to wet my whistle?'

Installed at the table with a cup of brandy-and-water in front of him, he leaned back so that his chair creaked alarmingly.

'So, what news?' Rooke asked.

'Ah, we are sad down at Government House. The governor and I. It is a blow, I will say. Perhaps you heard? The natives have gone, last night, slipped their fetters and made off.'

'Gone!'

'Sadly yes. Warungin had never reconciled himself to our company. Boinbar seemed happy enough—you remember, the taller cheerful chap. The governor is vastly disappointed. We were making excellent progress with the language.'

'Oh?'

Silk made a show of hesitating. Rooke recognised the signs that he was preparing a *bon mot*.

'Our friend Boinbar was quite the devil of a fellow, he was at pains to teach me the words for such important notions as pissing and shitting and the other thing as well. *Propagating the species* is how I decided to gloss it for the governor.'

Rooke laughed, thinking of the governor primly accepting this form of words.

'Other than those exceedingly useful notions we have an extensive vocabulary. We know, for instance, that the north wind is *boor-roo-way*.'

He separated the syllables out carefully.

'Wait, or was the north wind *bow-wan*?'

Silk pulled his notebook from his pocket and thumbed through the pages.

'I think we are not altogether sure, to tell the truth. But the east wind is *goniee-mah*. The sun is *co-ing*, a mouse is *bo-gul*, good is *bud-yer-i*. And we think that the suffix *–gal* means tribe. Or perhaps place.'

'Tribe, I see. Or perhaps place?'

If Silk heard any irony in this, he ignored it.

'Boinbar seems to distinguish something by the use of the suffix. He refers to himself as *Cadi-gal*, and then he points across the water and says something like *Cammera-gal*.'

'I see.'

'Well, Rooke, the governor and I were making considerable progress, but we would not pretend to be fluent as yet. His Excellency is confident, however, that there will be other opportunities. We treated them like kings, Rooke, did not of course let them guess at our shortness of supplies, and between them in a day they made short work of what would last us a week. Warungin would not touch anything but fish, but Boinbar tried everything and developed something of a taste for wine. We even taught him to toast the king, excessively amusing to see. We have every confidence that he will return before too long.'

Silk sat up at the table memorising the list of words, covering the English with a hand, staring up into the underside of Rooke's shingles.

'*Co-ing*, the sun. *Bo-gul*, a mouse,' he whispered to himself, a conscientious boy learning his lessons. '*Bud-yer-i*, good. *Budyeri*, good.'

He closed the notebook and stretched a leg out, ostentatiously at ease. Rooke knew something was coming.

'My intimacy with the native men, I have to tell you, Rooke, is of the most inestimable value for my little narrative. The whole story is excessively diverting. But I lack the beginning: how they were taken. Gardiner would not speak to me about it. It is far and away the most momentous event that has taken place in our time here! I need detail, I need the account of an eyewitness, but he would tell me nothing.'

He leaned forward across the table.

'What did you hear, Rooke, Gardiner must have spoken to you of it?'

Rooke drew back as if from heat, took advantage of the table wobbling to hide under it, adjusting the chock that kept it steady. When he came up again he had the words.

'Why, only that it was a complete success!'

He felt a flush coming to his cheeks. He had never learned the knack of lying. He got up and busied himself with some kindling.

'But Gardiner said nothing to you?' Silk demanded. 'At the time, or afterwards? Or at any time since the event took place?'

He would have made a good lawyer, Rooke thought.

'We speak of all manner of things,' he said, snapping a handful of twigs over his knee. 'We have in common an interest in the heavenly bodies, of course.'

He heard himself, Lieutenant Rooke at his least lively. Silk went on watching him. He felt the muscles around his mouth tense, straining to allow his face no expression whatsoever.

'Well,' Silk said. He sat smoothing his hair at the back, where it curled in a glossy wave over his collar.

Rooke could feel the pressure of his gaze, that wordless coaxing. He felt ugly in his skin, clumsy in his attempt to be secret. He wondered if writers of narratives could smell when there was more to a story than met the eye.

All Silk hungered for was a piquant addition to his narrative. But if he should get hold of the story the way Gardiner had told it in the privacy of the hut, and make it public, it would be a catastrophe.

The governor would be obliged to act. The colony did not have sufficient officers to hold a court-martial, but he would have Gardiner suspended from duties to live in a kind of blank until a ship arrived that could take him back to England to face judgment.

And then? Gardiner had not disobeyed, only regretted having obeyed. He would not be hanged. Probably. But His Majesty's service could not accommodate an officer who questioned an order. The best Gardiner could hope for would be to lose rank. That would be like losing a limb. Or he might be expelled in disgrace like those rebels in English Harbour. Whatever the outcome, Gardiner would spend the rest of his life a marked man.

'Really, Silk, you pay me a greater compliment than I deserve,' Rooke said. 'In thinking I might be aware of things. That you are not.'

Outside he could hear the white parrots gathering to roost in the tree on the side of the ridge. They swooped and cavorted with harsh squawks like creatures in pain.

I wish to God I had not done it. He had heard those words, and heard them with sympathy. That made him subject to their dangerous power. He must forget that he had ever heard them.

The settlement was nine months old, and the earliest date for the return of Dr Vickery's comet had arrived. Rooke had Dr Vickery's calculations: the comet would re-appear between October 1788 and March 1789.

Every night he groped his way up to the dome. He wished he had made the room a little bigger: with the quadrant on its rock and the telescope on its stand, there was not a great deal of room for an astronomer.

He had never yet seen a comet. He was four years too young to have seen Halley's and since then lack of instruments or cloud cover had prevented him observing those that had been discovered. Dr Vickery had showed him drawings of Halley's comet, but he could not believe that a glowing tail could light up half the sky, thought that the artists must have exaggerated.

Nothing was lighting up half the sky over Sydney Cove, New South Wales. Inch by inch Rooke scanned the arc in which Dr Vickery's calculations placed the comet. He took care, he did not hurry, he checked that the arc was correct. The first time he found a blur on the black sky, the heat of his excitement fogged the eyepiece and he had to wipe the lens clear, and take a few steadying breaths. He spent the next day in a state of suspension between hope and the determination not to hope, and when he found the object again the next night, he was glad he had not hoped too hard. The blur had not moved in relation to the stars around it. It was not a comet, just a nebula sent to tease him.

His days and nights became reversed. When dawn bleached the sky he went down the crooked steps to his living quarters and lay under the blanket on his stretcher, waiting for the day to pass in sleep and another night of observation to begin.

As October passed into November a long run of cloudy nights made observation impossible, but Rooke still spent most of the night awake, sitting in the dark watching for a break in the clouds. November passed into December and the sky cleared, but no comet appeared.

By Christmas he was frankly anxious. It had not occurred to him that he would not find the comet. He thought now that was an arrogance for which he was being punished. It was because of the comet that he was exempt from ordinary duties. That was the arrangement Dr Vickery had come to with Wyatt. It was the basis on which the governor had allowed him to stay out on the point with his musket gathering dust in the corner. If the comet were never found, where would that leave the astronomer but with his fellow officers, doing his duty with them?

Rooke visited the settlement only for the Sunday noon meal at the barracks, sitting half-asleep while talk washed around him: the supply ships had still not appeared, a man had been found dead of starvation, an examination by Dr Weymark had found his stomach to be quite empty. The vegetable gardens were robbed every night, Brugden was going further afield to find game but coming back with less. The natives had become bolder. Two prisoners out picking sweet-tea had been stoned. Another had vanished leaving only a hacked hat. A private had become lost in the woods and staggered into the settlement with a spear clean through his shoulder. The governor ordered that no one but Brugden and his fellow gamekeepers was to go into the woods under any pretext.

Some thought these attacks were a response to the kidnapping of the two men. Gosden and Timpson opined that the governor should not have ordered it done. Lennox and Willstead, on the contrary, considered that he should make a greater demonstration of force. Opinion was divided, but the result was clear: the guards had been reinforced and the marines were standing double shifts.

Rooke feared the governor would recall him from the point. *If there is to be no comet, Lieutenant,* he could imagine him saying, *then I must insist you take your turn.*

Rooke might have asked advice of Silk, but he did not trust a man whose narrative was so important to him. Instead he turned to Gardiner. Neither of them had ever referred to the day Gardiner had uttered the words that could ruin him. But between them now was a bond of trust.

'God, yes,' Gardiner exclaimed. 'No doubt about it, Rooke, we have got to get you that comet. Otherwise the governor will have you close up shop here.'

He brought up the old copy of *Barker's Treatise on Comets* from *Sirius* and the two of them sat companionably at the little table in the hut re-calculating the comet's probable track. Had Dr Vickery made a mistake? Neither Rooke nor Gardiner put the thought into words, but each knew the other shared a certain private glee in checking the Astronomer Royal's geometry.

Still the comet did not appear: not on the track predicted by Vickery, nor the slight variant worked out by Gardiner and Rooke. From the time the stars appeared at dusk until they faded at dawn Rooke peered through the telescope. During the day he tossed restlessly on his stretcher, sleeping only fitfully although exhausted, and woke at dusk unrefreshed. As January came and went, the face looking back from his shaving glass was haggard with searching.

Gardiner made the climb up from the settlement one afternoon as Rooke was readying the telescope for the night.

'Leave it, man. Look at you, I have never seen you so careworn. Leave it now and come out in the boat with me. Perfect tide for the whiting and I have got the boat just down here a ways.'

He took Rooke's arm, amiable but adamant, and Rooke yielded.

The sun was dipping low and a flood tide was swelling the port as Rooke took his place in the stern of the little skiff and Gardiner stroked easily along. In the lee of the closest island he heaved the anchor out. The two men sat in silence, their lines disappearing into the water over the stern.

Dusk was passing into night, the shape of the land a silhouette, the sky pure light with no colour, the water mysterious, shifting around the boat. Gardiner was right, Rooke thought, he had been looking into a dark tube for too long.

Gardiner suddenly yanked on his line and a fish arched through the air and into the boat.

'Three more like that and we will be shot of that damned salt junk. Or the unnamables that Brugden gets. Have a taste of this one, boys.'

He baited his hook with a slimy yellow mussel and threw the line out again.

'You might write to Dr Vickery,' he went on, as if it were part of the same thought. 'Give him some flummery, you will know what to say. As for the governor, well, something will turn up. But stay out of his way, I would, until it does.'

Gardiner caught four whiting, Rooke two. By the time he was making his way back up to the observatory Rooke was in a quieter frame of mind. He broiled his fish and ate them with his fingers, too hungry and tired to bother with the niceties, before sitting down at the little table, the candle close to the paper.

Reverend sir, Rooke wrote, *I have looked out every night for the comet at every favourable opportunity, but have not yet seen any thing of it; the weather indeed has been so constantly cloudy for these weeks past, particularly at night, that I have doubted whether it were not possible for it to have passed entirely without being seen; on the other hand when we have clear weather it generally lasts as long, with some intervals of cloudy, without being excessively so, or for a long time together.*

He was conscious of something wordy and obscuring about this sentence, but he folded the letter up. Heaven only knew when the ships would arrive that would take it to England. Before then, he hoped he would have better news. He would tear it up. No one need be told of failure if it were followed by success. But, as Gardiner had guessed, the act of writing had the effect of shifting his anxiety out of his mind and onto the paper.

The interlude in the soft light of the harbour had steadied him. For once he did not go up to the dome, but laid himself along his stretcher and drifted into sleep.

*

By April it was clear that, however an astronomer might do the calculations, no comet was going to appear. Rooke had been perched out on his point for nearly a year. He devised a new justification for remaining there with his instruments, and tried not to wonder how long it would serve him.

In the Northern Hemisphere it seemed natural, an aid to navigation provided by the Almighty, that the spot around which the imaginary northern axis of the earth rotated was marked by a brilliant star. In the south there was no such aid. To the naked eye the south celestial pole was an area of darkness.

As far as Rooke was concerned, the lack of a star in the south was one more reminder that, if there were an Almighty, he was not concerned with human convenience.

But there were, in fact, stars at the south celestial pole, visible through a telescope, and the Frenchman Lacaille had mapped them forty years before. When, as a student at the Academy, Rooke learned that Lacaille had died the very day he himself was born, he felt a bond to the man as if something had been handed on. Now he set himself the project of continuing where the other man had left off. Through the eyepiece he made out the constellation of *l'Octans Reflexion,* just as it was drawn on Lacaille's chart, and *Sigma Octantis* very faintly marking the spot where the world turned. But he could see stars in addition to those marked on Lacaille's chart.

Pricks of light that only an astronomer could see would butter no parsnips with the governor. His Excellency was not a scientist, did not value knowledge for its own sake. Still, Rooke worked away patiently with quadrant and micrometer, marking the location of each new discovery.

His measure of the months was no longer the small events and anniversaries of the settlement. Time for him was now the time of the heavens, watching each night as one constellation slipped out of sight behind the edge of the slit in his roof, and another appeared on the other side.

It was an eerie feeling, looking at stars that Dr Vickery had never seen, that even Dr Halley had never seen, that Hipparchus and Ptolemy could not have guessed at. Until a thing was seen, could it be said to exist? And if his eye through the telescope were the one that brought a certain star into existence, did not that make him a creator? In the back of his mind, in a place modesty would not allow him fully to visit, was even the possibility that he, Daniel Rooke, could connect the new stars he had found and, as Lacaille had done, give the new constellations names of his own devising.

Rooke could see so much more than Lacaille, with his now-obsolete instrument, ever had. It made him wonder whether in the future some telescope of unimaginable power would reveal even more stars, and still more after that, in the dark spaces between the ones he could see. There were nights when he almost drew back from the richness of the sky. Was there, in fact, no end to it? An end only to what could be seen?

PART THREE

The Names of Things

✳

When the drummer from the regiment came running down the rocks one afternoon midway through the second year of the settlement, Rooke watched him approaching with a blank heart. The lad would have a note in his breeches pocket. *Lieutenant Rooke, I do myself the honour of requesting your attendance at Government House tomorrow at nine o'clock.*

His reprieve was over, his time as creator of stars at an end.

But the boy was gabbling something, a message he had memorised and now recited woodenly, his face flushed like a girl's from his run up the hill. *From Captain Silk, sir, who sends his compliments and says, you will be interested to know the natives are come in, will you join him by the stream.*

As Rooke followed the boy past the hospital and along

beside the parade ground, he saw a group of three or four native men coming towards him. Close behind the men was Silk.

The contrast between the natives, clad only in their skins, and the captain in his breeches and jacket, was like a sum that did not add up. Silk did not look quite real, the braid and buttons on his red coat a filigree that bore no relationship to the chest beneath. No wonder the natives had needed proof that what lay under the covering was not a beetle or a bird, but a human being.

As he approached he could hear Silk trying out one of his words on the eldest of the natives, a lean man with a fuzz of grey hair on his chest.

'*Budyeri? Budyeri,* come on old fellow, let me know you have ears!'

The man did not respond.

'By God, Rooke, they are as loath to part with any speech as a miser with his gold!' Silk said. 'Good afternoon, by the by. I thought you would not want to miss this excitement. They began to come in last evening, Boinbar was the first, then others came, a few at a time. Warungin is here somewhere too. The governor agrees with me that it is clear they mean to stay among us.'

Rooke had never seen Silk so exhilarated.

'Come, Rooke, I do not intend to miss a second of this.'

He took Rooke's arm, following the natives as they moved away. They registered no astonishment at the houses, the rain barrels, the gang of shackled convicts. Rooke was reminded of seeing the Duke of Richmond and his party being shown the sights of Portsmouth. They had strolled along in just this way, looking to left and right with a mild benign indifference.

The grey-haired man went over to a hut. He did not knock on the door or hesitate on the threshold, he simply bowed his head to get under the low lintel and walked in, followed by the others.

Silk went over to get an angle of view inside and Rooke joined him. In the hut a woman stood by the fireplace, a baby clutched tight and two infants hiding their faces in her apron. She was as afraid as they were, but had nowhere to hide. The men moved around the room, picking things up—a teacup, a fork, a clay pipe—and putting them down, making quiet remarks to each other. One took up a piece of bread on the table and sniffed it. He dipped a finger into the mug of tea, licked it, grimaced. Another picked up a china plate, tapped it with a long hard nail, tested it with his teeth, set it down again.

This was the first time they had seen a teacup or a fork. The only time they would need to taste a china plate. It would never again be the first time. Rooke was aware of witnessing something unrepeatable and irreversible. He was watching one universe in the act of encountering another.

When they had had enough they turned to the doorway. Rooke and Silk moved back to let them pass. Up and down the street people were coming out of huts.

'The savages is come in!' Rooke heard a man call out of a

window. 'Quick Meg now and look!'

Brugden the gamekeeper stood in the middle of the street, legs apart, the musket over his shoulder and something furry dangling from his hand, watching the natives come towards him. When they caught sight of him they turned aside, whether because of him or by chance, Rooke could not guess.

They went over to the hut of a man Rooke knew, Barber by name and by trade. On a chair outside his door he had a private lathered up, a towel around his shoulders. He was standing behind him with his hand stopped in the act of drawing the razor through the white foam, staring at the naked men approaching him. The grey-haired one tilted his head and made a little gesture with his hand that said, *Kindly continue.* Barber began to stroke away at his customer's face, holding the tip of his nose in a finicky way so he would not move his head.

The natives followed every step of the procedure, and Rooke watched the natives. There was no sense in them of alarm or apprehension. It was as if the white men were strolling players putting on a performance for their entertainment.

Barber seemed to pick up something of that mood. When he had finished shaving the private, he whipped the towel away from the man's neck with a showman's flourish. The private sprang out of the chair and played up to the audience too, patting his cheeks clownishly to show the natives how smooth the skin was and inviting them to feel for themselves, which they declined to do.

Barber indicated by gestures that one of the men should sit in the chair. He held his towel ready. The man understood him perfectly, laughing and stroking his face where the black wool grew. He seemed tempted, but another man tested the keen edge of the steel on his thumb and could be seen to advise against it.

Willstead joined the small crowd.

'By God they are savage,' he said. 'Dirty too, look at the filth on them.'

Rooke watched the men catching Willstead's tone. The older one spoke a word or two and they all moved on.

'Well, Rooke,' Silk said, watching them go. 'At last, eh? I had quite exhausted the literary potential of brick making and road building. God willing, today marks the opening of a new chapter in the affairs of Sydney Cove.'

'Splendid,' Rooke said.

'At last, I can now go forward. Mr Debrett of Piccadilly will get his sparkling narrative after all.'

Rooke nodded, because that was what Silk expected. But he could not comprehend how a man could be presented with a moment as astonishing as a star moving out of its place, and see only the chance to make a story. He saw for the first time how different they truly were, he and Silk. Silk's impulse was to make the strange familiar, to transform it into well-shaped smooth phrases.

His own was to enter that strangeness and lose himself in it.

139

T he following morning Rooke stepped outside into the pearly dawn and saw two figures silhouetted against the sky: unmistakably natives, looking down towards his hut.

Since his encounter with the fishermen all those months ago, he had regretted his cheerful *Good afternoon!* and the silly social smile. He had planned another way to speak the language of welcome and now he tried it. He looked up at the men, a long gaze that said *I have seen you.* Then he sat against the wall of the hut, neither facing them nor turning his back. And waited.

He was impatient for them to approach. The urge to keep glancing towards them was hard to resist. Watching the clouds in the east lit up by the sun that was about to appear, he occupied his mind with speculating on what the top of the cloud might look like. Would it be rounded, as it appeared, or was that an effect of looking at it from below? After a time it was no longer a pretence: he truly forgot the men.

Then he became aware that they had come down the slope and were standing a short distance away. They still did not look at him, but nor did they stalk past. Moving his eyes but not his head, Rooke saw that one was Warungin.

Their eyes met, and the contact seemed to act as a signal. Warungin came forward and sat down near Rooke. With him, you might almost say.

Warungin put a hand out and said something. Said it again. Looked at Rooke as if waiting for him to say it. It seemed to start with a *b*, but there was a sort of thickening to the sound. Rooke made a stab at repeating the blur of syllables, but could not get his tongue around them.

Warungin said the word again. He was not making idle chat. He was doing a job of work, teaching a word to a man who could not hear it. Rooke tried again, copying the sounds like a snatch of melody.

'*Boourral*,' he heard himself say, a formless bubble of language such as an infant might make. Warungin said the word again, and Rooke tried once more.

'*Bere-wal.*'

Warungin nodded curtly, as if thinking, *as near as he is going to get*.

Then he began in dumb show to put a pocket telescope up

to his eye and peer through it. He must have used one, Rooke supposed. Perhaps during his captivity, along with the chairs and plates and glasses of wine the governor had offered him. One hand held the telescope, the other eased the tube in and out to focus, one eye looked steadily through the imaginary glass, the other was squeezed tight. He gestured—telescope, distant objects coming up close—and repeated the word.

Rooke put an invisible telescope up to his own eye, moved the tube in and out.

'*Berewal.*'

Warungin gestured impatiently with curved fingers, bringing the distance closer.

Not the object, but what the object did! *Berewal* was not *telescope*, but something like *a great distance off.*

'*Berewal,*' Rooke said again, and copied Warungin's gesture of scooping the distance towards him, eager to show that he was not so stupid, after all.

But Warungin was not interested in what an apt pupil Rooke was, did not smile or nod in praise. He pointed across the port to where the trees of the northern shore were catching the early golden light.

'*Cammera-gal,*' he said, slowly enough that Rooke could hear the separate parts. Then he laid a hand on his chest, over the lines of scars. '*Cadi-gal,*' he said. '*Cadi-gal.*'

That suffix Rooke remembered from Silk's list of words. *Gal: tribe, or perhaps place.* Warungin must be saying, *I am of the tribe or place called Cadi.*

Warungin leaned forward and put a hand on Rooke's chest, on the front of the red jacket.

'Berewal-gal,' he said.

He left his hand there, as if understanding could flow out of it, pass through the red wool, and into the heart of the man beneath. Rooke could feel it, the slight pressure of his hand against him. The first touch between two such separate beings. He almost expected a flash, as when lightning leapt between air and earth.

And with Warungin's hand on his red wool chest, Rooke understood. *Berewal,* a great distance off. *Gal,* tribe. Warungin was teaching him the name of his own people: *Berewal-gal,* the great-distance-off tribe.

He was pleased to have been named: it was a gift. But it was shocking, too. None of the mysterious belongings or impressive skills of the white men—the ships, the muskets that could split a shield, the telescopes, the gold braid—gave them any special standing. They were just one more tribe. *Berewalgal,* the great-distance-off people.

He hungered for more. How did you say, *Good morning, good afternoon, please, thank you, goodbye?* How did you say *Will you teach me your language?*

But once Warungin saw that he had been understood, he got up and turned his back, facing the ridge. He gave no sign, made no sound. But a group of natives filed into view and down the rocks: another two men, three women, three children.

They stopped in front of Rooke's hut and ignored him. He felt as if he were as unremarkable to them as any other part of the place: hut, rock, trees, man standing with his hands clasped in front of his privates like the reverend at prayer. He supposed these people did not expect much of a man who had to be taught even the name of his own tribe.

They were watching Warungin, who was delivering himself of a short speech. He pointed with his chin towards the hut, at Rooke, down to the settlement. He paid out his flow of words like a rope with knots in it: a piece, then a pause and another piece. Rooke felt his ears bulge out of his head with listening. Not just the words were opaque, even the cadence was unlike any language he had heard. Every phrase began emphatically and faded away. Trying to hear its form was like trying to take hold of running water.

Then all the men joined the one who had arrived with Warungin, sitting or squatting with their spears beside them. Rooke took a step in their direction. Should he join them? But one of the women, lean and wrinkled, her long dugs flaccid, her thighs fleshless, was walking towards the doorway of his hut. He made exaggerated ushering gestures. *Come in, welcome, I am pleased to see you!* He was glad there was no one there to watch him. The woman did not respond to the pantomime. Her dignity made his eagerness seem false.

She went into the hut and glanced around as if it were not

so very interesting. When she called back over her shoulder to the other women, a few curt syllables, they crowded inside. They inspected his domestic arrangements, murmuring to each other. One of them picked up a corner of the grey blanket over the bed and held it to her cheek, exclaiming, he thought, at the scratchy texture. They ran their long-fingered hands over the gleaming wood of the table, touched at the brass hinges where the legs folded. One lifted the cover of Montaigne and turned the pages.

He wondered if they were saying: *Look, he has bark here in a little square.*

Would they have the idea of square? Would some wild Euclid among them have pondered the marvels of the triangle?

Even in that tight space they had a remarkable way of not meeting his eye. They moved around him and he guessed that they were not speaking loudly because he was there. And yet he was not there.

The children had been hiding themselves behind the legs of the women, peeping around at Rooke and retreating if he looked at them. Now he caught the eye of a little boy, a sturdy fellow of five or six, who ducked back behind his mother's leg but then looked out again. Rooke smiled and even tried a wink, and by degrees the boy grew brave enough to dart out and touch one of the brass buttons on Rooke's jacket, dabbing at it as if it might be hot. Discovering that the button did not bite, he lost his shyness entirely, dancing around Rooke, plucking at his sleeve, pulling at his buttons and by the look of it shouting something to the effect of, *What are these? What are they for? Where did you get them? Can I have one?*

The women became bolder, holding things up to show each other as if exclaiming over goods at a market. They spoke to him, finding it hilarious to say the few words they must have already learned from the people in the settlement: 'Goodbye! Goodbye! How do you do! Mister! Missus!'

'Good morning, good morning,' Rooke replied, making them laugh even more. 'I do very well, thank you, and you?'

His shaving things lay on the table and one of the women— tall, full-figured, so magnificent in her nakedness that Rooke was a little shy—picked up his razor and bent it open. He sprang across the hut to snatch it away from her and all the amusement stopped on the instant. He tried to show them how sharp it was, cut a twig from beside the fire with the blade and kept up a stream of words—*sharp, you see, very sharp, it will cut anything, I use it to shave, see here?*—out of some instinct that speech was less frightening than silence.

The hut, ill lit at the best of times with its single window, grew dark. Rooke saw that clouds had gathered low and black, and it began to rain, fat drops hitting the shingles hard enough to make them rattle. A smell of cold mud rose up from the ground.

He went to the doorway and looked out. The rain hurled itself down against the rocks so violently it created a sort of spume. Under its force the bushes lashed about and the water of the harbour was almost invisible, the rain as thick as fog. He caught a few drops on his palm, held it out to his visitors.

'What is this, how do you say wet?'

The two young girls had hung back up till now, but one came forward and touched at his palm with the point of an index finger. Rooke looked into her face. She was perhaps ten or twelve years old, skinny and quick, with a long graceful neck and an expressive mobile face. He thought he saw in her the same impulses he was feeling himself: excitement tempered by wariness, the desire to explore held in check by the fear of making a wrong move.

She looked straight into his eyes and her mouth made a wry pout, equal parts frustration and amusement. He felt his own lips form an answering shape and saw her watching him—his eyes, his mouth, the look on his face—reading him in just the same way he was trying to read her.

She was like Anne had been at ten or twelve, was his instant thought. Dark skinned, naked, she was nothing like Anne, yet he recognised his sister in her: old enough to want to look into another's eyes, one human to another, and still young enough to be fearless.

She touched his palm again, this time with all her fingertips, stroking his skin as if to test its texture. Over the roar of the rain she said something. Like a deaf man, he watched her lips moving around the stream of words. Then she stopped and waited, her teeth resting on her lower lip in a way that said, more clearly than words, *Well? What do you make of that?*

He strained to separate some of the sounds, snatching at two that had surfaced clearly enough to be repeated.

'*Mar-ray,*' he tried.

She smiled, her entire face involved in the act. He had thought her eyes black, but now he saw they were the deepest brown. To look so freely into the eyes of another felt as dangerous as leaping from a height. He was amazed at such recklessness in himself.

'*Marray,*' she said again, pointing with her chin towards the rain. He noticed that Warungin and the men had gone, sheltering somewhere he supposed, and felt a host's pang that he had not called them in when the rain began.

Marray. What did it mean? Wet, something like that?

So close to her, with the water cascading over the shingles above the door and pouring onto the ground, it seemed awkward to say nothing.

'What a downpour,' he said, raising his voice against the din. 'Have you ever seen such weather?'

He listened ruefully to the drawing room sound of that. It was the sort of small talk he could seldom manage when it was appropriate, yet here he was, doing it as deftly as Silk might have, for an audience of six naked women and children with whom he shared, so far, one word.

Forthright, fearless, sure of herself, she looked to him like a girl who had already mastered whatever social skills her world might demand.

'*Paye-wallan-ill-la-be.*'

He could hear the way she was speaking slowly, making it easy for him. He tried to turn the sounds into syllables but could only get as far as the first few. She repeated each one and he said them after her. It was like being taken by the hand and helped step by step in the dark.

'*Paye-wallan-ill-la-be.*'

Even when he had it, it was not a perfect copy. There was something smothered or woolly, a slurring or legato quality to the word that he could not imitate. He could hear it, but his mouth did not know how to make it.

Still, everyone smiled and nodded at him and cried words that he assumed were along the lines of, *Well done! Congratulations!*

So that was the word, or perhaps words. But what did it, or they, mean? Something to do with the rain, but what, exactly? *What a downpour! Have you ever seen such weather?*

The rain eased and stopped as abruptly as it had begun. The little boy pushed past Rooke's legs and ran out. Two of the women followed more slowly. Rooke and the girl watched them splashing up the track, now a streaming torrent that gleamed in the rays of sun already emerging from the clouds.

'*Yen-narr-a-be,*' the girl said. '*Yennarrabe.*'

'*Yennarrabe,*' he repeated.

Her mouth twisted, perhaps in amusement at the way it

sounded. They said it to each other a few times. For the moment it was enough to pass the echo backwards and forwards. Even without knowing their meaning, the fact of exchanging words was a kind of message: *I wish to speak with you.*

The girl's face was so expressive, the sense of her personality so vivid, that Rooke's instinct was to take a step back and look away. But he did not. The old woman had made herself at home, puffing at the coals to bring the fire back to life, taking the twigs that the other young girl was handing her from Rooke's wood basket. With a reckless sense of taking a leap, Rooke laid the palm of his hand on his chest, where Warungin had laid his.

'Rooke,' he said. 'Daniel Rooke.'

She caught on straight away and made a good approximation of his name. Then she put her hand flat on her own bony chest. Uttered a few syllables he could not properly catch.

'*Ta-ra,*' he tried.

Over at the fire the other girl laughed behind her hand and he heard her mimic his effort.

He rolled his eyes, grimaced. *Yes, what an idiot I am, but harmless.*

He tried again and the girl went slowly until the shapeless sound resolved itself into syllables: *Ta-ga-ran.*

The word he was making was still not quite the same as the one she had said. But he saw her face open with the pleasure of hearing her name in his foreign mouth, and at having been the one to teach him.

150

Her name and those two other utterances were in his mind now, but, as sounds not connected to anything, they would soon lose their shape in his memory. They were not *Wind* or *Weather* or *Barometer*, but like those, these words were part of the climate of the place, data that ought to be recorded.

He got down an unused notebook from the shelf, felt the girl watching as he sat at the table, dipped the pen in the ink and opened the book. On the first page, in his neatest astronomer's hand, he wrote: *Tagaran, the name of a girl. Marray, wet. Paye wallan ill la be*—he hesitated—*concerning heavy rain.*

He read the words back to her, his finger under each syllable, stumbling through. She smiled, her face transformed, every part of it involved in the great beam of delight.

The old woman was calling out something. It might have been, *Come, children, time to go, time to go,* because she and the two girls left soon after. At the foot of the rocks, Tagaran turned.

'*Yenioo! Yenioo!*' she called, and he called back.

'Goodbye! Goodbye!' What else could she have meant?

'Come again,' he called. 'Come again soon, you are always welcome!'

But they were gone. He was farewelling the bushes tossing in the breeze.

✳

Small though it was, the hut seemed larger and emptier when they had gone. There was Montaigne on the bed where the women had turned its pages. There was the blanket, crumpled from where the majestic one had held it up to her cheek.

In the silence, the dripping of water from the roof was very loud.

'*Marray*, wet,' he said aloud. '*Paye wallan ill la be*, concerning heavy rain.'

He drew a neat line across the page underneath the words. It said, *This is all I know*. Below, the space of white paper waited. He thought of Silk's similar notebook, his similar, though more extensive, list of words. *Budyeri*, good. *Bogul*, a mouse.

But language was more than a list of words, more than a collection of fragments all jumbled together like a box of nuts and bolts. Language was a machine. To make it work, each part had to be understood in relation to all the other parts.

That required someone who could do more than collect words and learn them by rote. It required someone who could dismantle the machine, see how it worked, and put it to use: a man of system, a man of science.

Looking at the words he had written, he knew—in the way he knew a prime when he saw it—that he was that man.

And everything in his life had been leading here. He saw it as clearly as a map, the map of his life and his character. He had been born with the urge to understand how things worked. He could read in five languages. The unknown was his daily bread: astronomy was a profession of mysteries. Difference held no fear for him. He knew that strangeness was commonplace when you inhabited it.

Above all, his temperament suited him to the task. Those qualities that made him such a diffident social being were the very ones that equipped him perfectly for listening.

He knew, with as much certainty as he knew his own name, that this would be his proper work in New South Wales: to acquire the native language.

Having gone so far in his mind, he went further, and allowed himself to picture the day when he would brush his jacket and set off down to the governor's house with the notebooks in his hand. *Sir,* he would say. Perhaps it should be *Your Excellency.* Silk said that the governor liked to be addressed with his title. Perhaps he should ask Silk to go with him as a sort of ambassador.

Sir, Lieutenant Rooke seems to have found the basis on which the native language is founded!

In fact there would be no *seems* about it, but a certain modesty was becoming to a mere second lieutenant. Once the governor was paying attention, Rooke would find his voice.

I am pleased to be able to tell you, sir, that I am now able to speak with the natives such that a fruitful intercourse may be commenced.

The governor would be astonished. It was hard to picture that face expressing excitement, admiration, awe, but how could he not be excited, admiring and full of awe? Rooke would be presenting him not only with the means for the governor to fulfil his own ambitions in New South Wales, but with something

153

bigger. The governor would be the first to learn of an addition to the world's sum of knowledge almost as dramatic as Galileo's or Kepler's. *The earth moves around the sun. Gravity is a force that operates at a distance.* The journey of discovery he had just embarked on was of that order of significance, a journey not simply into the language of a race of people hitherto unknown, but into the cosmos they inhabited: the ways they organised their society and the gods they worshipped, their thoughts and hopes, their fears and passions.

After such a leap of learning, the world would no longer be the same.

✳

The first problem was not one of meaning but of music: how to convey in the familiar twenty-six letters those alien sounds. Thinking out the way to start was like stretching a muscle that had been unused too long.

He turned over the first page of the notebook. Those first entries had given him the beginning, but they were not the way he meant to continue. On the inviting field of the following page drew up four columns: *Letter. Name. Sound. As in the English word.*

He felt a thrill, a physical thing, anticipation like an appetite.

He was reminded of what he had not thought of for years, his old copy of Lily's *Grammar of the Latin Tongue*: the worn maroon cover, watermarked as with dark clouds, the spine that was coming away from the binding—his father had got it cheap from a stall at Southsea—and the woodcut in the frontispiece of men picking fruit with grand studied gestures.

Recklessly he turned over page after page of the notebook, heading each with a letter of the alphabet as Lily had done: *Native Tongue to English,* then again for *English to Native Tongue.*

Now he took a second notebook and on its flyleaf he wrote: *Grammatical Forms of the Language of N. S. Wales.* Words were all very well, but with nothing more than words one was forever a child, piping out the names of things. Grammar was the gearing that made them useful.

To begin with, he would have to limit himself to actions that could be acted out: *to eat, to go or walk, to drink, to yawn, to creep.* Foreign they might be, but these people must walk and drink, eat and yawn and creep.

He had better start modestly, with the indicative mood. *I eat. You eat. He, she or it eats.* Nothing much could be communicated without a sense of past and future, so he had better try for that too: *I will eat, you will eat. I have eaten, you have eaten.* And of course he must gather the useful imperative: *Eat!*

On the left-hand side of the page he wrote the English. Beside each entry were the spaces that would be filled, word by systematic word, with the unknown tongue. He headed the page opposite the empty verb templates with a title he hoped might gather up some of what was missing: *other inflexions of the same verb.*

He laid the notebooks out side by side on the table. The *Vocabulary*, the *Grammatical Forms*. The books were like the jaws of some ingenious machine. Between them they would crack open the nut of this language.

It would be an extraordinary task. Even Kepler, even Newton, had not been presented with a *tabula rasa* but had built on other men's work. Unlike them, he would be setting off to meet the unknown with only his ears, his pen and these little notebooks.

Rooke was aware of a tightness in his chest that was new to him. It took him some time to recognise that this was how it felt to be in the grip of a vision. Destiny was a grand word, but perhaps not too grand for what lay ahead.

*

The natives did not return for nearly a week. Rooke busied himself with the rain gauge and the barometer, wrote up his notes on the south celestial pole in a fair hand. He filled his kettle, he gathered wood for his fire. But as he worked he was watching from the corner of his eye for a movement at the top of the ridge. Branches fooled him, and the swift shadows of clouds. He would straighten up and begin a wave, and the ridge would mock him in its emptiness.

So when they arrived at last, he was half angry. But the little boy leapt down the rocks in his eagerness to reach Rooke and started pouring out a stream of words.

Rooke could not go on being haughty. After all, had they made him any promises?

The women came down the rocks slowly, babies on their hips, and behind them were the girls: the shy one, and the other one, Tagaran.

'Good afternoon! Good afternoon!' he cried. 'I am glad to see you again!'

It was just a form of words, he had said them a thousand times. But he meant them now in a way he had not on most other occasions.

The women had brought a piece of smouldering wood with them and set about lighting a fire near the hut. They moved in such a leisurely way, almost absent-mindedly, talking to each other, that it seemed the thing would never work—surely those pieces of wood were too large, surely that kindling was too far from the smoking stick? One woman bent down and blew—so briefly, he did not think it would have any effect—but shortly there was a fire and they sat down around it, the babies in their laps, sinking into the ground as if planting themselves.

The children came into the hut, the boy shouting at Rooke as though he would understand words said loudly enough.

'Well, yes, my young friend,' Rooke said, 'but I wonder if you will give me some words one by one? Will you tell me what this is?'

He pointed at his ear, but the boy covered his fine teeth with a hand, bending himself in two in hilarity. The girls called out to each other, a muddle of words in which he could not fix a single individual sound. It seemed that these children were too young and too cheerful to be useful to a man who needed conversation one syllable at a time.

The girl Tagaran was over at the table where the sextant sat out of its box. She reached for it and he put out a hand to stop her, flushing with the fear of it coming to harm. Courteous as a lady in a drawing room, she drew back. She turned to him and spoke with a question in her tone.

'Sextant,' he said. 'It's a sextant.'

With thumb and finger he made a circle around his eye and peered up through it. She watched gravely and followed his gaze to the shingles.

'No, not there,' he said. 'For measuring the vertical angle between the horizon and a celestial body. Such as the sun. For instance. Or the moon.'

She watched his words trail away.

'Daniel Rooke,' he said, 'at your service, and you'—he pointed to her—'you are Tagaran. But who are your friends, what are their names?'

He pointed at the boy and the girl, and Tagaran saw what he wanted. She spoke to the girl, gesturing towards Rooke, who bowed and pointed to himself.

'Daniel Rooke.'

But the girl could not seem to look at him, much less answer. Surely he was not frightening?

But perhaps he was. Large, male, a stranger, and clad in incomprehensible coverings: flaps and folds and bulges and

159

puckers of a tissue that was soft like skin, but not skin.

The girl murmured some syllables, more or less into her armpit.

'Again, if you please?'

Tagaran saw the difficulty. '*Wo-ro-gan. Worogan*,' she said.

She had already caught onto the need to articulate a new word one clear sound at a time.

The boy had no fear whatsoever. He jumped up and down in front of Rooke, bursting to be next. He tried: said something, but much too quick. Tagaran spoke to him and he said it again, but he could not go slowly enough. At last Rooke got it: *Bon-e-da*.

He opened the book at the page where he had written *Tagaran, the name of a girl*, and dipped the pen in the ink. Tagaran was watching every movement of this operation with the close attention of someone playing the cup-and-walnut game. He wrote: *Worogan, the name of a girl. Boneda, the name of a boy*.

She showed him that she wanted to try the pen, so he helped her dip it in the ink. Her hand was small and bony, hard in his own. She drew five small neat marks on the page, then another two sideways.

The boy exclaimed at the way the black marks appeared on the paper, but did not want to try. Worogan would not even come close enough to see, as if the pen held a dangerous power.

He had planned to start his vocabulary with *Parts of the*

Human Body. He pointed at his head and made a questioning face.

'Perhaps you will tell me,' he said. 'What is this, what do you call this?'

Tagaran understood immediately.

'*Kubbura.*'

She repeated it until he was able to write it down and read it back. Going almost too fast for him to keep up, she pointed to various parts of her head and face, so that in short order he had the words for mouth, forehead, eyebrow, even eyelash. But there seemed to be distinctions in her language that English did not bother with. As well as *kubbura* there was *ngulu*, forehead, *kamura*, top head, and *kuru*, which he translated as hind head although he knew that English had no such word except for the name of a deep-laned muddy village between Portsmouth and Greenwich.

He was eager to move on to arms and legs, feet and hands, but he thought Boneda and Worogan were becoming weary of the minute demarcations of the human body. Fearful of losing them, he picked up a piece of bread and made to eat it and straight away Tagaran said a word that sounded like *patadjiumi*: presumably, *you eat* or *you are eating*. He gave the bread to her and motioned for her to eat it. Like him, she only feigned, and said *patadjiu*, which he understood to be *I am eating*.

Oh, she was quick.

A conjugated language then, and the root possibly something like *pata*. There was a swollen feeling in his chest as if he needed room to breathe. In one leap he had gone beyond the simple exchange of word for thing, word for action. Here was his first principle of the grammar, the first means of connecting and articulating!

He leaned away from the table beaming at Tagaran. She beamed back. Clearly she was enjoying this as much as he was.

Then, to everyone's extreme amusement, he acted out the other verbs he had already made the blanks for. He walked, he drank, he yawned and sneezed and pinched.

Worogan forgot to be shy, so entertaining was Rooke's performance. By the time he was creeping on all fours they were staggering with laughter, their dark cheeks slick with tears, Boneda almost crowing, unable to catch his breath.

Rooke collapsed on the dirt. He was laughing so uncontrollably at the picture of himself creeping that he had given himself a pain in his side. How odd it was that he should finally learn how to play the fool, and become the child he had never been in his childhood, in the company of these three children with whom he shared hardly a word.

It was turning into a warm afternoon and he could feel the fleas, enlivened by the heat, nipping him in his jacket. The children watched the business of ridding each arm of the sleeves and peeling the thing off. When a flea jumped out they took the coat from him, flipping the fabric around, until they caught it and cracked it between their nails.

Looking at Tagaran, Rooke made his fingers spring off the coat.

'*Burudu*,' she said.

He was still writing this down under *B: burudu, a flea*, when Tagaran picked up the jacket and said a few words, he guessed, *What do you call this?*

'Jacket. That is a jacket.'

She nodded once, and went through the action of taking off a garment.

'*Minyin bunilbangadyimi jacket?*'

He heard with surprise how quickly she had adopted the foreign word. And she must be asking, *Why are you taking off your jacket?*

'To rid it of fleas,' he said. '*Burudu.*'

'*Ah, Burudin!*'

Her question was answered, she was ready to go on. But he gave a guffaw of excitement that made her stop. He knew now that this language was not only conjugated but its noun forms were inflected too, like Latin and Greek. *Burudu* was flea, and *burudin* seemed to be *because of the fleas*, some form of the ablative case.

Was this what Galileo had felt, turning his telescope to the night sky and seeing stars that no one had seen before?

It was like a dance between the two of them, or the voices

of a fugue. He pushed it further, taking the jacket from Tagaran, and shrugged it back on in order to take it off again.

'Now, how might you describe what I just did, I wonder,' he said. 'Since you have no jackets, what words might you use?'

He did not expect her to understand, but she copied his action with her own imaginary jacket, movement by movement: peeling back the opening on both sides, pushing the right shoulder up, reaching around with the left hand to tug at the cuff of the right sleeve.

'*Bunilbanga.*'

He repeated the sounds, made to write them down, but she stopped him.

She mimed putting the jacket on.

'*Banga,*' she said, and looked to make sure he understood.

Then she took the imaginary jacket off again. It was as if she had spent her life removing jackets from her narrow body.

'*Buni.*'

With a shock like a fright, Rooke realised that *banga* must be a word like *to make* or *to do* or *to put*—like *faire* or *machen* perhaps, he could clarify that later—and *buni* or *bunil* must be a negating or reversing principle. At this rate, he would be fluent in a month!

'*Bunilbanga jacket,*' he said, for the pleasure of feeling the words in his mouth. Her face in repose was made stern by the heavy brows, the prominent cheekbones, the deep-set eyes, but was transformed by her smile.

'*Budyeri karaga,*' she said, splitting the words off from one another so that he understood.

Karaga, mouth. And *budyeri* was one of Silk's words. She was saying *good mouth*, which could surely only have the sense of *you speak well*.

What an astonishing thing, that her praise filled his heart.

The sun was sinking, the women were gathering up their babies, calling to the children. Worogan and Boneda went after them, and Tagaran was about to follow, but he held out a hand to stop her.

'Tomorrow?'

He made hand-over-hand gestures.

'You will come again tomorrow?'

She did as he had, speaking and making gestures. He hoped she was saying, *Yes, I understand, I will return tomorrow*. When they had come to the end of gesturing they looked at each other. He opened his mouth, there was something he wanted to say to her, but what could he tell her, and in any case how would she understand?

Then Worogan called to her from the rocks, she turned and shouted back, and the moment was gone.

He waved from the doorway.

'Goodbye! Goodbye!'

They all called the word: the women, the girls, the boy. Even after they had disappeared beyond the rocks, he could still hear Boneda's clear voice: *Goodbye, goodbye, goodbye!*

Taking off his shoes that night, he saw even by firelight how dirty his feet were, each toe ringed with a dark halo. It was the shoes that did that, he realised. The toes of the natives, as straight as fingers on a hand, were not dirty. The dust must fall off their feet rather than be trapped by footwear.

As he got the basin and warmed some water in the kettle, he thought what a marvellous symmetry there was to the whole business. If you had the convenience of shoes, you also had the convenience of basins of warm water. But if you lacked shoes, you also lacked the dirt that made the basins of warm water necessary.

What was the word for *foot*? Next time he would ask Tagaran. And then he had better ask for the plural, in case it was as irregular in her tongue as it was in his own. He imagined himself earnestly showing what a quick pupil he was, announcing *foots!* She and Worogan had a way of not looking at each other, studying the ground, that he was beginning to suspect was their courteous means of not laughing at him.

He lay down and brought the candle close so he could read. *He that shall tax me with ignorance, shall have no great victory at my hands. As I am, so I goe on plodding.*

Montaigne would be enjoying it here, he thought, almost as much as he was himself.

*

The idea of tomorrow was clearly an elastic concept among the Cadigal. A week passed, and Rooke's first visitor was Silk. His urbane face for once was creased with vexation.

'Lennox has done his time at the Rose Hill garrison,' he said without preliminary. 'Done more than his time, and is loud in pointing out that fact to the governor.'

Rooke felt he must have missed something.

'Time? Lennox?'

'Yes, and that poor devil Gosden is in a consumptive decline, he has not left his bed for two weeks—which leaves no other captain of marines but myself! Can you believe it!'

'Ah, yes?'

'Rose Hill, Rooke, for God's sake, Rose Hill must have a

captain, and unless His Excellency swiftly taps you or one of the other lieutenants, there is no one other than me. Lennox says he has done more than his fair share for the breadbasket of the colony. I have to grant him that, the farms have flourished under his stewardship.'

Beyond the doorway Rooke could see a sliver of the path. He found himself hoping the natives would not choose this time to visit.

'His Excellency agrees that it is unfortunate,' Silk went on. 'But it is as he says, his hands are tied, he cannot send a man of lower rank.'

'But you know, Silk. It may be worth, well, a promotion.'

'Yes,' Silk said without enthusiasm. 'It may be. I hope so. I think it likely.'

A year before, Rooke knew he would have had a pang of envy at the thought. Rank: in a remote way he knew it mattered, but now it seemed bloodless and irrelevant.

'I cannot refuse, I can only hope not to be rusticated there for too long. My narrative is coming along apace, I am gathering speed with it and with all due humility I must say that in parts it is—well, I can only use the word *sparkling*. But at Rose Hill I will be sadly lacking in matter. What of interest could possibly happen with a hundred dull prisoners grubbing at the ground and twenty even duller privates guarding them?'

A thought occurred to him and his mood turned a corner.

'Unless, of course, there should be an uprising of the

prisoners, or an attack by the natives!'

His tone said the idea was absurd.

This was the point when it would be natural to say, *Oh, by the way, Silk, speaking of natives, I had a visit from some the other day.*

He took the breath to say it, but did not speak. What had occurred the other day was more than just *a visit from some natives.* He did not know what it was, or why he did not want to share it. Only that it was private. Something between himself and Tagaran was exploring its nature. If it had to grow under the gaze of Silk he feared it would be stillborn.

'For your sake, I hope there is no uprising. Or attack,' Rooke said. 'I hope only a quick return is forthcoming. To civilisation.'

But if Rooke was honest with himself, it was not *hope* that he was feeling. It was relief. He would have his peninsula, and whatever might take place on it, to himself.

Silk had not noticed his friend rehearsing words he did not say. Having finished with Rose Hill, he now remembered something else.

'I suppose you know that *Sirius* is to be sent to Norfolk Island for a time? With your friend Lieutenant Gardiner, of course.'

'Norfolk Island?' Rooke was shocked. 'Gardiner? Sent there?'

'Why yes,' Silk said. 'Captain Barton is to sail tomorrow. The place is evidently more fertile, *Sirius* is to carry some prisoners away to reduce the burden here…I have no doubt you will miss Gardiner, but my word Rooke, you look as if you had seen a ghost!'

'Yes,' Rooke said. 'That is, no. That is, I am taken by surprise, that is all.'

He told himself, *Gardiner is a lieutenant of the navy, his ship is sailing to Norfolk Island.* It was an ordinary task in his profession. It was not banishment, it was not punishment.

But in his mind he was aware that two ideas had melted together, the way things did in dreams: Gardiner's dangerous outspokenness and what felt like exile.

'For myself, too, it is disappointing,' Silk was saying. 'As you know, I was hoping to persuade the good lieutenant to speak of that episode in which he had a part. But, like you, Rooke, he has a knack of disappearing from view.'

Disappearing from view. He had congratulated himself on having managed that, but this news about Gardiner reminded him how hollow that achievement could be. He had let himself drift in his mind some distance from *serving and obeying.* He had allowed himself to feel he was his own man, taking hold of this new place with both hands, opening all its doors himself.

But New South Wales was not an open door, and he was not his own man. New South Wales was the possession of King George the Third. The commission he had given his governor awarded James Gilbert sovereignty over every man black or white, every object great or small, and every relationship of whatever sort that might take place in his kingdom.

Rooke was not conscious of having planned his actions, but it seemed that he intended to keep to himself the events that were happening in the isolation of his point: the visits, the notebooks, his sense of having been offered a gift. But concealment might have consequences. He did not know what they might be, but, as he watched Silk walk away up the path, he knew that this paradise, like any other, was finite.

R ooke had learned some of the names of the women who visited with the children. At least, he thought the words he used were their names. Barringan was the fine tall woman who had come to the hut on the first day and was Boneda's mother, or perhaps his aunt, he had never got that quite straight. The old woman, clearly a person of authority, was named Mauberry, but Rooke privately thought of her as Nanna, because her cut-and-dried certainty about everything, as well as a wry humorous look, reminded him of his grand-mother.

These women, and others who came only now and then, greeted him when they arrived but then established themselves with the babies around the fire some distance away. They busied themselves making fishhooks from curved shells, and fishing cords from bark. They held the stringy fibre up and named it for him—*dturaduralang*—mostly, he suspected, to laugh at the way he tried to say it.

He remembered his sisters as babies, but they were always swaddled in garments and wrappers like parcels, lying in the wooden cradle with only their faces and fingers showing. As far as he knew, they had never sprawled naked across their mother's bare thighs as these infants did. It had shocked him the first time, but now he wondered whether this was what a lap was for: to make a living cradle so that a child could abandon itself to sleep.

On some days it was Warungin who led the little procession down the rocks. The children kept at a distance while he sat with Rooke on the ground outside the hut. Sometimes it might be half an hour before Warungin said a word. If Rooke tried out some of his new vocabulary, or held up an object wanting to know its name, Warungin would make a minute adjustment of his position but say nothing. He did not seem to find silence awkward.

For Rooke it was like looking into a peculiar sort of mirror. Among his own kind, he was the one who made others uneasy with his silences. It was humbling to learn how to do nothing more than sit.

Sometimes Warungin arrived with other men. Then Rooke sat like a child, wordless and ignored, while they talked too fast for him to catch any sound that made a word he knew. In the company of other men, Warungin lost his sternness, and embarked on extended stories for the entertainment of the others. He was a mimic of great accuracy. More than once Rooke recognised Major Wyatt, his bristling indignation perfectly captured, or poor Gosden with his nagging cough.

He wondered whether Warungin also entertained the men with an imitation of the way Mr Rooke's mouth groped for the shape that would make some new word.

Now and then Warungin arrived ready to give Rooke a language lesson. He laid out on the ground all his tools and weapons: the barbed spear, the smooth-tipped spear, the four-pronged fishgig, the sword-like length of wood with the oyster shell gummed into the end. Item by item, he taught Rooke the names. *Dooul,* the spear with two barbs. *Wudang,* the bone point of a spear. *Yelga,* the barb of a spear. *Yara,* to sharpen the points of a *muting* or fishgig. Rooke had his notebook beside him, his pencil in his hand. He knew, by some indication he could not put his finger on, that Warungin did not approve of the writing-down business. But he was patient, repeating the words and holding up the objects until his pupil understood.

When he gathered the weapons and stood to leave, the children came over. Tagaran, Worogan and Boneda were nearly always there, and sometimes two other girls confusingly alike and possibly sisters, called Tugear and Ngalgear. There had been such hilarity at his attempts to sort out the two that Boneda actually wet himself. Rooke was interested to see that this caused no embarrassment. It was simply the crowning touch to the comedy, and a tribute to it.

He sat with Warungin as a pupil, he exchanged a few words with the women out of courtesy, he enjoyed the company of the children, but it was with Tagaran that he had conversations. She never came to see him by herself, but the other children soon tired of the games with words the two of them played. They had no patience with the way Rooke was not content to understand, but had to have a thing repeated often enough to write it down. After a time the others drifted away and left Rooke and Tagaran alone together.

Somehow, he did not quite know when it happened, she gave him a name, *kamara*. It meant *my friend*, he gathered, something of that kind. He did not know whether she had heard the English using the word *comrade*, or whether by chance the words were alike in the two tongues. There was so much he did not know.

Tagaran was the eldest of the children, but that was not the only reason she was so clearly their leader. In every situation in his life, Rooke had seen that there were people with a power of personality that gave them effortless authority. It was not to do with rank or position: the governor lacked it. Rooke did not possess it either, he knew that about himself, but Silk had it, and so did Gardiner.

And so did Tagaran. It was more than intelligence, though Tagaran's understanding was like quicksilver. It was more than assertiveness, though he watched her rapping out orders to the other children. It was a quality of fearless engagement with the world.

She never tired of giving him words, or of learning the English in exchange. Like Warungin, she was a vivid mimic and seemed to love the moment of seeing him understand.

When a baby cried over at the fire with the women, she explained *breado tunga,* she cries for bread. When Rooke gave her some—the greater part of his dinner, but he did not tell her that he would go hungry—to take to the child, she pulled out the dough with a word he understood to mean *soft, easy for a child to eat,* as opposed to the rock-like crust which she explained was *hard, in the sense of difficult to break.*

Tagaran gave him the words for *belly,* for *back,* for *skin,* for a *boil* on his arm, another that might have been *finger* or *fingers* or *hand.* He learnt the word for *grass* and for *sand,* or perhaps it was *dust* or *dry earth.* He wrote down the words that seemed to mean *what,* or *what's this,* as she held up his clasp knife, and the words that seemed to be *show it me,* or *let me see,* when he opened it and then closed it. When Boneda trolled a block of wood along the ground and the other children threw pebbles at it, she told him it was *karagadyera.* The block? The action of trolling? He was not sure, but wrote down the word.

He abandoned system, using a pencil for greater speed, scribbling *open the door* and *I set it on fire* and *the armpit,* or perhaps it was *to tickle;* Tagaran and Worogan were laughing too much to explain. In his haste he jotted down only as much of the English as would let him remember later what he intended. When the talk turned to the sun—Tagaran complaining that he was shading her from its warmth—out of habit he jotted down the astronomer's circle-with-dot. Under the press of so many words, his pencil split and she watched with the closest attention as he bound it together with string.

It was not the way he was used to working. Even the swiftest planet gave a man plenty of time to be sure, and to be neat. To work like this, not stopping to think, was a giddy exhilaration like drunkenness.

Language went in both directions. Without the benefit of notebooks or pencils repaired with string, the natives not only knew many words of English, but had already made them part of their own tongue, altering them as their grammar required. *Bread* was now *breado*, not simply borrowed but possessed.

When he heard himself do the same thing one day he felt as if another boundary had been left behind. Warungin, in teaching mode, had brought along one of the throwing sticks called *womera*. He showed Rooke how he had recently replaced the shell blade—the *kaadian*—gummed into the end. *Kaadianmadiou*, he said, and Rooke wrote it down: *kaadianmadiou, I kaadianed it.* Having written it, he realised what he had done. *I kaadianed it:* a sentence hitherto unknown to English. He was not simply learning another language. He was re-making his own.

A boundary was being crossed and erased. Like ink in water, one language was melting into another.

✳

Tagaran ran into the hut one afternoon, goose-pimpled all over, drops of water sparkling on her skin and in her hair. Rooke got up from the table but she pushed at him with a wet hand.

'*Ngyinadyiminga!*'

He could see that she was saying, *You stand between me and the fire!* and got out of her way. She turned around and around in front of the flames, shivering, a purple tinge to her lips. He threw on more wood and blew at the fire until it blazed.

'*Bogidiou,*' she said, and he thought automatically, from *bogi*, to bathe or swim, therefore, probably *I bathed or have been bathing.*

'My dear child, it is not weather for bathing!'

He knew she could not have understood precisely, but saw that she caught the tone: a big brother who thought he knew best. Just as Anne would, on being advised to wear her warmer but uglier shawl on a cold morning, she gave him an exasperated look.

The fire was roaring in the chimney, but she was still shivering, so he took his jacket from its peg and put it around her. For an instant he felt her narrow shoulders under his hands, felt the life of her, her breathing self, right next to him. Then she twirled like someone dancing a minuet, taking hold of the collar of the jacket as she did and handing it back to him.

Straight away he regretted that momentary touch on her shoulders. He might think of her as his sister, but Tagaran was not his sister. He wanted to explain, *I have a younger sister you remind me of.* But then thought, was that enough to justify such familiarity? If some native man, Warungin for instance, had come up so close to Anne, and put his hands on her shoulders, what would he feel?

He stepped back.

'I am sorry.'

It was perhaps not too late to rescue the moment. He hung the jacket on its peg, taking rather more time than the action required, and took up a position near the door, as far from her as the hut allowed.

She performed another turn in front of the fire and stopped with her back to it, looking at him. He saw her thinking, her eyes going to the jacket hanging against the wall, the man standing with his arms folded at the other end of the room.

'*Goredyu tagarin,*' she said, and went through a performance which included the fire, and the jacket, and herself shivering, from which he understood her to mean that she would become warm more quickly if she remained naked.

Which was correct, he realised, and showed more understanding of the logic of wet skin and the heat of a fire than did his own world of endless garments. Her explanation told him why she had twirled herself out of what had almost been an embrace. But he saw that she was explaining something else too. She had seen his unease and understood its cause.

Still he felt awkward. In fact, he knew he was blushing. He could feel the warmth coursing through his blood, beating out against the skin. He turned to the table and made something of a to-do of getting the notebook and pen out and writing.

Goredyu tagarin, I more it (that is, I take more of it) from cold. That is to take off the cold. At this time Tagaran was standing by the fire naked, and I wished her to put on clothes, on which she said, Goredyu tagarin, the full meaning of which is, I will or do remain longer naked in order to get warm sooner, as the fire is felt better without clothes than if it had to penetrate through them.

This was longwinded, but by the time he had finished, his blush had subsided and Tagaran was no longer shivering.

She went with him to the small hollow he had cut below where water seeped out of the rock. Rooke dipped and poured, and when Boneda ran up, wanting to know what was going on, he let him dip and pour until the kettle was full. In the hut he put the kettle on the fire and the children saw straight away that he needed more twigs—they knew the same thing his grand-mother had told him, *little sticks burn the hottest*—and they had the fire blazing and the water heated in short order.

He took it outside to the stump on which his enamel basin sat next to the rain gauge. He had wedged a stick upright into the stump and jammed his looking-glass into its split end, and now began the ritual of shaving, which never failed to entertain the children: the stropping of the blade on the leather strap, the making of lather with the shaving brush, the way the lopsided mirror caused him to tilt his head to one side as he drew the blade through the white foam. Worogan pointed to his nose, bare of lather.

'*Minyin bial kanga?*' she asked, why don't you wash this part?

Worogan was laughing sideways at Tagaran. She had lost her shyness, and now he saw that there was some private joke on the subject of his shaving, or his nose, or the whole business of being cheeky to a man, or to a white man. He pushed his tongue into his cheek to tighten it for the blade, peering into the insufficient mirror. He knew he would never learn what the joke was, but he smiled, mostly with his eyes to avoid getting soap in his mouth.

When he had finished shaving he folded up the razor, wiped his face with the towel, and tossed the water out. Tagaran picked up the kettle and shook it, indicating there was a little left, and by gesture asked his permission to pour the water into the basin, then she plunged her own narrow hands into it. Against the white enamel of the basin her skin was sumptuously dark. He put his own hand down alongside hers: pink, somewhat freckled, unfinished looking, he thought, by comparison.

He took her hands in his and laved them with the soap and, to complete her toilette, he wet the corner of the towel and wiped her face. She watched him as he worked. Further than her face he was shy to go: a face was a public thing but a body, no matter how childish, was private.

He gave her the towel.

'Wash, come, wash yourself.'

She took the towel and dipped the corner in the warm water as she had seen him do.

Watching her—her face showing every nuance of expression: surprise at the unaccustomed feel of warm water on her skin, wariness, the fun of doing this new thing—he risked a joke.

'If you wash yourself often you will become white!'

He did not know whether she would understand the words, or his attempt to translate them into actions, making to wash his forearm and then holding it beside hers, the white skin against the brown. He thought it a good joke, the sort of absurdity a child would appreciate, and all the more entertaining because his own skin was so dead-looking compared to hers.

But she rubbed at her forearm with the towel a few times, inspected it, and flung down the towel in a pet.

'*Tyerabarrbowaryaou!*'

He supposed she was saying something like *I shall not become white!*

She stuck out her bottom lip, pouted and postured, acting out despair. He was appalled, cursed himself for such a badly judged bit of tomfoolery.

Then she winked at him, and he saw that she was not acting,

but overacting. He had made a promise as a joke, and she had taken hold of the joke and run further with it, giving it another twist that compounded its ironies.

When she saw his face clear with relief, she left off pouting and laughed with pleasure at what they had made together. He laughed too, astonished at it, so rich and layered.

But it left a taint of something else, a sense of the ease with which a thing could go wrong. He must be careful, he told himself. The rapport between them was easy, but he must not make assumptions. There was too much to lose, and not just the glory of being the first to speak the native tongue.

Afternoon was wearing into evening. Over by the fire, the women were picking up the babies and calling to the children. But Tagaran and Worogan were talking together and glancing at Rooke. Some scheme was afoot.

'*Matigarabangun nangaba,*' Tagaran said, and gestured, palm under cheek, finger pointing to the floor at her feet.

Nangaba: in that he could hear a familiar word, *nanga*, the infinitive of the verb *to sleep*. He already knew *nangadiou*, I slept, and *nangadiemi*, you slept. Was *nangaba* the future tense? Was Tagaran suggesting that she and Worogan sleep in the hut?

He went over to Mauberry and Barringan at the fire, trying to explain, to ask, to confirm the rightness of it. Yes, they agreed, Worogan and Tagaran would sleep in the hut of Mr Rooke. There was much hilarity. He had no hope of following their shouted comments but was pretty sure that they were about him.

It was perhaps as well that he did not understand.

The novelty of spending the night in an unfamiliar place was something he recognised. Perhaps that was universal among children. Even he had begged to spend the night under a canvas awning in the slip of garden behind the house in Church Street.

Until recently Daniel Rooke had felt all of a piece with the child he remembered himself to be. Now that little boy seemed an entirely different person from the man waving goodbye to a group of laughing naked women and their plump brown babies with no more sense of the strangeness of the scene than if they were his neighbours in Portsmouth.

He shared his food with the girls, although he thought they ate more for the novelty of it than any pleasure. Indeed, there was not much pleasure to be got out of stale bread and a little broiled salt pork. But he made sweet-tea—they exclaimed at the fact that he put the leathery leaves in the kettle and steeped them—and he understood them to say that they used the leaves too, and gave him the name of the plant, or perhaps the leaves, or perhaps the infusion: *warraburra*. They thought that to drink it out of teacups was the most amusing and extraordinary thing.

He sipped his own cup of *warraburra*. He had grown more fond of it than real tea, enjoying the way its faintly aniseed, faintly astringent, faintly sweet taste left him refreshed, his spirits somehow clearer.

It was the oddest pleasure to have these two staying with him. Had he ever played host before? He could not think of an occasion. He had expected many things of New South Wales, but not that he would learn to keep house and entertain guests.

Where in the hut did they wish to sleep? In front of the fireplace, of course. Worogan lay down on the mat he had there and curled herself towards the warmth, but Tagaran pointed to the blanket on the bed, unmistakably a command, so he spread it out for them on the floor. Worogan was not sure, but Tagaran made her get up so they could lie on it together. She was such a bossy child! He hoped he would never find it necessary to refuse her anything.

They curled up side by side, and he sat at his table and opened his notebook, turning to *W* and recording *warraburra, sweet-tea.*

But Tagaran sat up.

'*Boobanga,*' she said. '*Boobanga kamara!*'

He saw from her actions, that this was a request: *Cover me with a blanket, my friend!*

He did not think she would like the feel of the rough wool against her skin, so unused to any covering, but he was not going to try to explain. Tagaran would have to find out for herself about blankets, just as he had discovered for himself, that night under the canvas awning, that it was cosier in the house. His father might have had the same contradictory feelings as he did now: a longing to protect, and an imperative to stand aside.

He took his second blanket and laid it over the two girls. He had not been comfortable under the canvas in the garden at Church Street, but comfort was not the point. The point was that Tagaran wanted to feel the very texture of the white man's world.

The girls lay quietly and he went back to the notebook. How would he record the joke that he and this child had shared earlier in the afternoon?

Tyerabarrbowaryaou, he wrote, *meaning, I shall not become white.*

That might be correct, but it did not begin to capture what had happened.

This was said by Tagaran, he added, *after I told her if she washed herself she would become white, at the same time throwing down the towel as in despair.*

This was an improvement over the bare translation, but left out all that was important about the moment. What had passed between Tagaran and himself had gone far beyond *vocabulary* or *grammatical forms.* It was the heart of talking; not just the words and not just the meaning, but the way in which two people had found common ground and begun to discover the true names of things.

But how did you write down truth in a notebook, when the truth was far more than the words or the actions? When, even in English, he would not know how to express the thing that had passed between them?

To somehow convey that drama on a page, he supposed he

would have to do as Silk would. He would have to be willing to go beyond the literal, to take words into some place where they were no longer simply descriptive, but had a life of their own.

Well, he was not Silk. These words could carry none of the life of the exchange. The only reason for recording them was that they would allow him to remember. For the rest of his life he could read these words and be transported back to this *here*, this *now*. This happiness.

He got his greatcoat down from its peg, stretched himself under it on the bed, and took up Montaigne. *Of Thumbs*. He had read his few books so often he almost knew them by heart, but he always enjoyed *Of Thumbs*.

At night the hut always felt as if lost on the edge of space. Surreptitious scratchings and rustlings from outside had the effect of deepening the silence and intensifying his solitude. There were nights out here when he lay in the dark feeling as if he were the only human on the face of the earth.

With the girls alongside him, the space within the walls was transformed. The embers of the fire cast a steady radiance. Tonight, as never before, the hut was a cosy vessel coasting along on the currents of night.

He had chosen the place with solitude in mind but he was pleased, for once, not to be alone. Perhaps he was not, after all, such a solitary soul. That was something about himself that he had not known before. Had it always been there, but never brought to life by the right circumstance? Or was something in the air of New South Wales changing him?

He had only read a page about thumbs when he saw Tagaran raise herself up on an elbow and call softly to him, *kamara*, her face creased with sleepiness.

'*Minyin bial nangadyimi?*' he said carefully. Why don't you sleep?

'*Nyimang blanket, kamara,*' she answered.

Did she say, *Put out the blanket?* It was as he had thought. He got up and began to pull the blanket away. Worogan slept on, but Tagaran grabbed it and glared at him in surprise and indignation. He watched her face register a cascade of thoughts.

'*Kandulin!*' she said and pointed. Candle!

It was the light that was keeping her awake.

It was so unlike her to make a mistake in speaking that he made a joke of it, bending down towards the blanket and puffing as if to blow it out. She smiled, acknowledging the game.

'*Tariadyaou,*' she whispered.

He recognised the form of the past tense, and some part of a word he thought meant something like *mistake*. Was she saying, *I made a mistake in speaking*?

'Yes,' he whispered back, looking down at her face, very childlike with the blanket around it. 'But you know, to err is human.'

His father had said such things to him, in just the tender tone he heard in his own voice now. She could not understand those last words, he thought, but she closed her eyes for sleep.

He arranged himself under his coat again and blew out the candle, smiling at the idea of *putting out the blanket*. It was unlike Tagaran to make a mistake, but it was equally unlike himself to think to turn a mistake into a joke.

Well, it might be unlike Lieutenant Daniel Rooke, but for the person she called *kamara* it seemed to come as naturally as breathing. *Kamara* must have existed all this time, he thought, but without the remarkable chance of the arrival of Tagaran, he would still be voiceless.

He lay on his side listening to the soft sounds of the embers creaking and collapsing, and the girls' innocent unaware breathing. He could see the curve of their joined silhouette swelling and subsiding. One of Tagaran's arms was flung out from beneath the blanket, the hand palm-up, the fingers loosely curled around air.

He felt—what was it?—a warmth was it, in his chest? He could not locate it or name it, but knew it was to do with Tagaran being under his roof, that trusting hand turned up towards him.

The light from the embers had faded to nothing. The hut was as dark as blindness. In a short time he knew that a full moon would rise. As he had done on so many other nights, he got up and wrapped himself in the greatcoat. Tonight he would not watch the moon as an astronomer, but as any other man might who could not sleep. He felt his way over to his table and the shelf above it, got the brandy bottle, poured a glass mostly by sound, and took it outside.

The world was darkness upon blackness. Only the harbour was a different, shifting blackness. No one but an astronomer who knew where to look would have seen the modest glow on the horizon. He waited, used to sitting in the dark until a light appeared in the sky where he knew it must. The brandy warmed him: poor brandy, he tasted the harshness of it, but it was a pleasure he did not often allow himself.

The merest sliver of moon was a line of light along the horizon. As he watched, it rose until all but the last fraction of its circumference was free. It spread out along the horizon and seemed to flatten itself, clinging to the earth as if reluctant to rise.

It was simply an effect of the atmosphere, but how odd and interesting that the human mind should be so constructed as to find it a thing of beauty. Knowledge of why it happened only made the sight more lovely. He was willing to sit transfixed, the mosquitoes whining around his ears, until the instant where the stretched liquid parted and let the moon sail alone through indigo space.

Tagaran had praised him again that day: *kamara budyeri karaga*, she had said, *kamara* speaks well. He liked the way she called him *kamara*.

There was a particular sly mocking glance that she shot sideways at him when he was being slow. Other than his sister, Tagaran was the only human in the world who trusted him to be able to laugh at himself.

Perhaps this was what it was like to have children of one's own, and move with them in an atmosphere of easy playfulness. He supposed that one day, like most men, he would marry. If he did, and had those unimaginable children of his own, he would remember this. He tried to picture himself telling them the story. *Then one night the two native children slept in my hut.*

He thought there might not be any words for what was happening between himself and Tagaran. Like the language of the *Cadigal* that he was learning, word by half-understood word, the language of his feelings for her was beyond his reach. He could only step forward blindly, in trust.

Perhaps it was the brandy, but in the eerie wash of moonlight he sat content to the point of euphoria.

From Rose Hill, Silk sent Rooke messages to the effect that the breadbasket of the colony was even quieter and stupider than he had feared, and that all he had to show for those weeks was an understanding of clod moulding, information he would just as soon have gone to his grave without. If the governor did not soon send for him, he wrote, he would be forced to come down with some painless but disabling ailment in order to rejoin the human race in Sydney Cove.

In Silk's hands, even the complete absence of material in itself became material. Rooke read his notes and wondered if Silk had made a copy for his narrative. Or would he expect Rooke to keep his correspondence?

He had just dismissed the messenger when another arrived to summon him to the parade ground. A prisoner had been caught digging up potatoes in the government garden and secreting them under his coat. He was to be flogged.

Rooke knew that the settlement could not tolerate the theft of food. No one could argue with that. But hunger was beginning to dominate everyone's days. The prisoner women had scoured the shoreline around the bays, picking off every limpet and winkle, but were still pale and scrawny, their eyes dull. The only person in the settlement that Rooke had seen still looking robust was the gamekeeper, Brugden. Out in the woods, who was watching if the hunter ate what he shot rather than bring it back for the communal pot?

As for this poor devil who had taken the potatoes, well, man was an organism that demanded food. To take food when it was available was—purely in scientific terms—a correct response to hunger.

The hard-faced judgment that called the action *theft* and demanded punishment was another matter.

As a servant of His Majesty it was justice Rooke was obliged to obey, but he wished the prisoner had not stolen the potatoes. Had not tried to hide them under his coat. Above all, that he had not been caught.

The man was very fair, his curly hair shining like wire in the sun, the skin of his back so white as to be almost luminous. And gleaming: the poor wretch was sweating. His body knew what was coming.

All the marines were obliged to be present, and most of the

prisoners. What was the point of punishment if no one saw it? Warungin was there too, standing beside the governor and glancing about. Rooke supposed this must be part of his education. There was British civilisation, in the form of china plates and toasts to the king, and there was British justice.

Warungin was unconcerned, only interested. Unlike everyone else present, he did not know what he was about to see.

A thought occurred to Rooke. He slid his eyes around while keeping his head at the regulation angle. With the intensity of prayer he hoped that he would not see Tagaran watching from behind the trees, wondering at this unusual gathering of the *Berewalgal.*

And if she were? If he caught sight of her, peeping out from behind a tree with that look she had, avid for knowledge? Would he break ranks, go over to her—somehow make her understand that she must leave, cover her eyes, block her ears—while the ranks of other redcoats looked on?

He stood at attention with his musket at the slope. He was already sweating in his jacket, his heart was thudding, and the thing had not yet started.

He was close enough to hear the governor explaining to Warungin, pointing towards the thief lashed to the triangle in the bright empty space where the ground beat back the light.

'A bad man. Stole food.'

Warungin watched the words form on the governor's lips.

'This man took food that did not belong to him.'

Warungin nodded, whether with real understanding Rooke could not say.

'So we punish.' The governor was determined to be clear. 'Every man is the same. If he steals, he is punished.'

It was interesting to hear that magnificent idea—the product of hundreds of years of British civilisation—spelled out so plain.

Then the flogger came out onto the patch of sandy ground. He shook out the cat, separating the tails, thwacked the butt into his palm once or twice.

Even the birds seemed to have fallen silent.

Rooke set himself to thinking of the muscles in his back. How ingenious was the mechanism of the spine, that could hold the body upright no matter what was going on in its head. He thought of his feet. Such small balancing points, and yet they knew how to stop him toppling. He imagined a carved replica of himself, complete with musket, jacket and wooden face, standing on a base as narrow as his feet. Would it fall over? He thought of the way the ground was pressing up against the soles of his shoes. Or rather the way his feet were pressing down into the ground. That was gravity. It was the tremendous hand that kept the cosmos in its place. Kepler had got close to understanding, Newton had snared it in words. *Every particle of matter in the universe attracts every other particle.*

Rooke was performing a species of magic, or trying to. He

was removing himself from the place and time he occupied, while leaving his body there staring into the middle distance, musket at the correct angle.

At the first sickening crack of the knots against the skin, the prisoner cried out, but so did someone else. Rooke saw Warungin trying to rush forward, shouting at the flogger, his face distorted. He strained against the governor holding him back and looked wildly around at the marines in their ranks. He met Rooke's eyes and shouted to him, some word over and over. Across the space between them it was one man begging another.

Lieutenant Rooke looked away. He stiffened his neck further back into his collar, gripped the butt of his musket more tightly. He could feel the sweat slimy on the wood. His collar was choking him, his cap was squeezing his head, his jacket seemed made of iron. *Stop, stop, stop,* was the only word his brain could produce. *Stop,* to Warungin, to make him not go on calling to him. *Stop,* to the flogger, to drop the whip, walk away. *Stop,* to the governor, to take pity on all of them.

He clenched his hand around the gun, squeezed up his toes in his shoes. He was a stone, a piece of wood, a replica of a man.

Wyatt and Weymark on either side had got hold of Warungin's arms. Between the inhuman noises the prisoner made at each stroke, Rooke could hear the governor continuing to work away at explanation.

'Bad,' Rooke heard. 'Bad man. Thief.'

The governor's face pinched up, trying to make Warungin understand.

'Took food. Stole food that was not his food.'

Warungin had stopped struggling but his face was turned away from where a man's back was methodically being reduced to red pulp. Rooke could see the powerful tendons in his neck straining. At each stroke and each cry from the prisoner, Warungin flinched.

This was justice: impartial, blind, noble. The horror of the punishment was the proof of its impartiality. If it did not hurt, it was not justice. That was what the governor was trying to convey, but the noble concepts evaporated in the light.

Rooke heard the shocking wet slap of the cat landing on split flesh, twenty times, thirty times, fifty times. At each stroke, the man's body convulsed against the ropes that held him to the triangle. The flogger had to stop and comb his fingers through the tails of the whip after each lash to clear the flesh that clogged them.

The prisoner endured seventy-four lashes before his body sagged from the ropes. It was Surgeon Weymark's job to judge whether the wretch had taken all he could on this occasion. He barely touched the man's wrist in a gesture of taking his pulse before nodding that, yes, he had had enough, cut him down.

A hundred and twenty-six lashes left for next time. Rooke thought that the idea of that waiting for you might be worse than the present pain.

Even when the man was cut down and dragged off, Warungin's mouth was still a peculiar strained shape. There was a grey overlay, like a dusting of ash, to the brown skin of his face. He was staring down. Rooke thought he might be about to vomit.

The governor touched his arm.

'It is over, my friend,' Rooke heard him begin.

But at his touch Warungin flung up his arm as if the governor's hand were red-hot.

'Let us return to my house, I will give you something to eat,' the governor said.

Warungin did not reply, did not look at the governor or any of the other assembled *Berewalgal*. He did not even glance at Rooke. As soon as Wyatt released him he turned his back and walked away. Rooke watched him go, this man with whom he had sat cross-legged on the ground.

Warungin was not thinking *punishment, justice, impartial*. All he could see was that the *Berewalgal* had gathered in their best clothes to inflict pain beyond imagining on one of their own. Seen through his eyes, this ceremony was not an unfortunate but necessary part of the grand machine of civilisation. It looked like a choice. When those fine abstractions fell away, all that remained was cruelty.

And Rooke had been part of it. He had not cried out with horror or rushed forward to put an end to it. He had looked away when Warungin called to him.

Chosen to look away. No one had held him there. He had made that choice, because he was a lieutenant in His Majesty's Marine Force.

There it was, in the very words. Force was his job. If he was a soldier, he was as much a part of that cruelty as the man who had wielded the whip.

*

ilk was at last recalled from Rose Hill at the beginning of summer. He was full of the dreariness of the place.

'Listen to this, Rooke, you had better sit down, otherwise you are likely to fall over from excitement. Listen: *Dod says he expects this year's crop of wheat and barley to yield full 400 bushels.* Have you ever heard anything so scintillating?'

'But you will make something of it. Turn, you know, a sow's ear…'

'Oh, no talk of sows, if you please! I have to admit, though, that the place had its charms in spite of its dullness. They have cleared a great deal of ground, and from the top of the hill I was struck by how grand and capacious the prospect seemed, after not seeing an opening in the woods of that extent for such a long time.'

He felt in his pocket for his pencil.

'I must remember that, it was a striking and novel sensation.'

Rooke watched him write, thinking of his own threadbare notes in his own small book. How might he begin the task of telling Silk about what had been happening on the point?

'And what have you been up to, Rooke?' Silk asked at last. 'Has there been anything of note to report?'

Silk was hardly waiting for an answer, he was so sure there had been nothing *of note to report.*

'Well,' Rooke began.

He must tell, otherwise what up till now had been simply private would take on the dangerous power of a secret. The task was to tell, but to minimise. To reveal, but reveal something so small and so dull that Silk would not pause to examine it.

But while he was assembling words and rejecting them, Silk was fiddling with the things on the table, and came across the blue notebooks, insufficiently hidden under Montaigne.

'*Grammatical Forms of the Language of N.S.Wales,*' he read. 'Why, look here, I believe you have been making a study of the native tongue. Oh, and *Vocabulary of N.S.Wales.* May I...?'

He had his thumbs ready to spread open one of the little books, only his unfailing courtesy demanding he go through the motions of asking permission. Rooke cursed himself for not hiding them properly. With Gardiner and Silk both gone, and no other visitors from the settlement likely, he had forgotten to be careful. He realised he had never pictured another eye looking at the words he had written, and could not think quickly enough how to say, *No, Silk, do not open it.*

'I think you will find not much of interest,' he said. 'My researches are, you know, in a very preliminary...Were there natives at Rose Hill? Any encounters?'

For a moment he thought the ruse had worked.

'Why yes, I had almost forgot to tell you,' Silk said, putting the book down, although keeping his hand on it. 'While I was there a hut was burned to the ground, luckily empty. Some time later a man out hoeing ground was attacked, a spear in fact pierced the ground between his feet, but by good fortune he was not struck.'

Rooke watched Silk's thumb absently stroking the edge of the book, where the blue cloth was worn.

'There is trouble brewing, is my feeling, but what to do when the attackers will not let themselves be seen? The governor plans to send another ten men and one of the small cannons. The Rose Hill redoubt is superbly positioned. A dozen men could fight off any force of natives.'

Rooke had hoped for a diversion, but had not expected this. The small dramas taking place in his hut had filled his horizon. Out in the greater world of His Majesty's penal settlement, it was apparent that other sorts of events were beginning to rumble, and his ignorance was dangerous.

While he was talking, Silk had again picked up the book

and seemed to feel he had sufficient permission to open it.

'Ah yes, I have this myself, if you remember. See this here, *budyeri*, my spelling differs from yours, but the word is clearly the same. And look, here is *bial*, meaning no, although I felt that a double e made the pronunciation less open to error. But look at all these pages! My word, Rooke, you have had your nose to the grindstone.'

Rooke reached for the book, but Silk was still turning through the pages and would not yield it.

'No, Rooke, there is no need to be modest, this is a considerable achievement. You must learn not to hide your light under a bushel, my friend!'

He leaned back, closing the book on his finger but keeping a grip on it. Rooke told himself that his unhappiness at Silk reading his notes was a remnant of all the other idiosyncrasies which he had to conquer. He would have to accept that privacy was a luxury his life did not offer. If his time of being alone with the natives had come to an end, he supposed he must accept it gracefully.

'You know, do you not,' Silk said, 'that I was hoping to have a chapter on the language in my narrative?'

Perhaps his tone was more challenging than he had intended, and he followed it up with a somewhat windy laugh.

'May I ask what you are planning to do with these *Grammatical Forms*? Will you publish?'

Silk was moving too fast for Rooke.

'Publish? Publish this?'

'Well, in that way your labours would find a wider audience, would they not?'

How different Silk was from himself, Rooke thought. Silk could imagine no use for words other than reaching an audience. Why would a man labour, if not to publish? Until recently he himself would have viewed things the same way. Would have leapt at the idea of his endeavours having a public readership.

In deciding to learn the language of the natives, he had thought to take a single step: to write down the words. Now he saw how far he had travelled from the world he once shared with Silk. Tagaran seemed to have led the way down some other road altogether.

'There may be some interest. Among scholars. Who might collect the languages of far-flung tribes. Publish—I do not, I would not think, I fear there may not be an extensive number. Of readers.'

He saw something in Silk relax, as if he had succeeded in getting a dead weight up to the top of a slope and could let gravity do the rest.

'Absolutely, Rooke,' he said. 'I have to concur. Probably not of much general interest. And my grief is that I have so little of the language here, in part because of my sojourn at Rose Hill. I am as it were thinking aloud here, you realise.'

He hesitated, but Rooke wondered whether the hesitation

was merely a piece of theatre.

'It occurs to me, Rooke,' Silk said, as if just arriving at the thought, 'it occurs to me that we might be able to enter into a partnership, you and I. What say you add your vocabularies and your grammatical forms to my own journal—with full credit to you, naturally—in the form of an appendix?'

He did not wait for Rooke to reply but hurried on.

'Needless to say, you would share what Mr Debrett has promised me—we can come to some arrangement as to that—a proportion of the amount on a *pro rata* basis.'

He paused. Rooke could only think of one word: *No!* but said nothing. Silk hurried on.

'By which I mean of course that if, say, your contribution, in terms of numbers of pages, was a sixteenth of the whole, then you would have one sixteenth of the profit...what do you say, my friend?'

'Yes, well, I know what *pro rata* means, Silk, thank you.'

'Why, Rooke!' Silk's jocularity was a little forced. 'Are you haggling with me? Believe me, we will come to an arrangement that will suit you. You will get a fair share, you may be sure of that.'

Something in Rooke caught alight the way a twist of tinder did, a quick white flare.

'It is not about my share, Silk! I am not haggling with you over the pounds, shillings and pence!'

Those two notebooks recorded the best of his life. Perhaps

he would be obliged to share them, but they would never be a matter of profit.

Silk was leaning forward across the table watching Rooke's face. Just as he had on the day he had wanted to know about Gardiner, Silk was catching a whiff of something hidden.

'Well, there may not be enough,' Rooke said. 'To show. In the end. Let us wait and see. Shall we?'

He reached over the table for the books and got one, but Silk was leafing through the other.

'I will hold you to that, Rooke,' he said absently, and Rooke thought, *Hold me to what? I have promised nothing.* Silk turned another page, and Rooke saw his narrow face quicken with surprise.

'*Tya*-something or other…Go on Rooke, what is it?'

Rooke could not do other than oblige.

'*Tyerabarrbowaryaou.*'

'Thank you, and here is the meaning: I shall not become white. *This was said by Tagra…*' He stumbled on the name, tried again. '*Tagaran—after I told her if she washed herself she would become white, at the same time throwing down the towel as in despair.* Such a sad little picture, Rooke. Surely it was cruel to make her such a promise?'

'No, no, it was spoke in jest! Both, we both spoke in jest. It was a joke. That the white people think their skin superior…'

The white people. He was speaking as if he were not one of them.

'It was spoke in jest,' he said again, but heard the hopelessness in his voice. 'She is a clever child, she is not so silly as to believe…We enjoyed the joke of it.'

He had written *as in despair* in order to indicate that her despair was feigned. To him it had obviously been a joke. What native, even a child, would believe that washing would make them white? He had failed to record the joke on the page, in the same way he failed to note that they were breathing, or that their hearts were beating.

Silk was not listening.

'My word, Rooke, you have certainly made considerable headway, and perhaps not only with grammatical forms!' He held the book to the light from the window and read. *'Goredyu tagarin, I more it (that is I take more of it) from cold. That is, to take off the cold. At this time Tagaran was standing by the fire naked, and I desired her to put on clothes.'*

It was his own arrogance as a man of science to have so precisely written down every detail of that small event so charged with delicate feeling. Stupidity, too, to have carefully formed every letter in his clear hand, so any eye in the world could read it.

'A child, you say? I hesitate to contradict you, my friend, but listen to this: *Wana* something-or-other, you will not have me, you don't want my company? This must be you, Rooke, and here is the answer: *Wana*-something-or-other else, I don't desire your company.'

His animated face was full of surprise, admiration and—could it be?—something like envy.

'My word, but you are ahead of the rest of us here. Are Mrs Butcher's beauties not enough for you? What a sly dog you are!'

A sly dog? Rooke did not know what Silk could be talking about, and then he did. He heard the words again in Silk's voice, had a picture of Tagaran—some leering, grotesque Tagaran—flaunting herself at him. He felt himself flushing, a wave of heat that rose from his neck into his face, his ears, his scalp.

'No! No, no!'

Silk smiled, watching him with an inviting quirk of the eyebrow. The story was almost visibly forming about him: *Our quiet friend Mr Rooke and his little friend Tagaran.*

Calm, Rooke told himself. Calm at all costs, or the story would be graven in stone.

'No, no, you misunderstand. What you read there. She was not speaking to me but to another child.' In trying to be casual, his voice had become husky. 'Some of them come now and then. To beg food from me. And so on.'

This was surely dull enough, and not even a lie.

'I myself had no part in the exchange other than recording it. They were having an argument. One was going off. In a huff. But came back later.'

He was explaining too much. Silk was watching, smiling, his legs crossed, jerking one knee up and down so his foot bounced, waiting for silence to do its job.

'One of them has proved herself to be an excellent tutor of the language.'

One of them. It was to protect Tagaran, but it was a betrayal. Tagaran was not *one* of any of *them*. She was herself, unique in every particle.

'My dear Rooke,' Silk said at his most urbane, 'there is no need to explain. We are both men of the world.'

Men of the world! If he had been a man of the world he would have seen how those words could be read. A man of the world would never have been so fatally innocent as to write them down.

In Silk's mind there could be no intimacy with a native girl that was not physical. And how can I hope to persuade him otherwise, Rooke thought, when I myself do not understand and have no word for that intimacy?

I should have known, he cursed himself. *Should have remembered his nose for a secret.*

He had lived in that place that seemed so different as to be inviolable. He had drifted along without time or space or consequence. Everything had been suspended while he and Tagaran floated in some corner of the cosmos in which the impossible could unfold. Now the iron laws of time and place were asserting themselves.

Not speaking had made things worse. He could see that now. Made it look furtive, when there was nothing to hide.

'They have an artless charm, the girls, I grant you,' Silk said. 'And an admirable lack of coquetry. But Rooke, as a friend, might I just utter a word of warning? Hidden away out here, you may not be completely aware, well, the natives are—let me put it this way, the governor is concerned. Those attacks at Rose Hill…You might think to go a little carefully.'

'Thank you, Silk,' Rooke said. 'It is kind of you to speak as a friend.'

Kind, but what could Silk know, reading his words through a lens of prurience, and making guesses that were so wrong as to be sickening?

He took the notebooks from Silk, got up and put them away on the shelf. Once up there between Lacaille's *Stelliferum* and the *Nautical Almanac*, they were invisible. So small, like the first snag in a stocking, that could hardly be detected, that seemed not to have any importance. By the time the snag had unravelled the whole thing, it was too late to mend.

✳

The earth travelled elegantly along its orbit, tilted on its axis—somewhat like the governor, Rooke thought—bearing the settlement into the full heat of summer. A week had passed since his meeting with Silk, but something in Rooke was still reverberating, a disturbance in the air, a tremor in his sense of himself.

He heard them before he saw them—*Kamara! Kamara!*—Tagaran with Tugear and Worogan, almost falling down the rocks in their haste to reach the hut. No one else, none of the women, none of the other children. Just these three, landing at his door in the afternoon, breathless and crying.

'Heavens, what has happened, what is wrong?'

Tagaran was in disarray as he had never seen her, her face wet with tears, her mouth shaking, air heaving raggedly in and out. She was trembling like a horse after a gallop. He saw brilliant red blood on her arm and her side.

She panted out a stream of words, he could not understand a single one.

'Get in, girls, get in by the fire!'

He spread a blanket for them to sit on, threw sticks on the fire. He had little enough in the hut, but poured them each a cup of water, found the hard old slab of biscuit that was to have been his meagre supper and gave them each a piece, leaving himself a mouthful. Tugear was sobbing, would not taste the water or the biscuit, sat with her knees up to her shoulders.

Tagaran took a deep breath to try to calm her breathing and was racked by an enormous hiccough, then another. She smiled crookedly and started to say something, hiccoughed again, and all at once the crisis was over, Tugear laughing and banging Tagaran on the back until she angled her elbow up to make her stop.

'Now tell me, girls. What has happened? What is this about?'

Tugear and Worogan looked at Tagaran. She spoke, but too fast. He caught *white man*, all the rest was a blur.

'I cannot understand you,' he said. '*Mapiadyimi.*'

'*Piyidyangala whitemana ngalari Tugearna,*' Tagaran repeated, one word at a time for his benefit.

In *piyidyangala* Rooke could hear a stem he knew, *piyi* to beat.

Even as his brain was computing the meaning, his heart was shrinking. *A white man beat Tugear.* He did not have to unravel all the implications of this to know that it was something he did not want to hear.

Tagaran was energetically acting out an angry face, a hand rising and falling. He could see it all, only too clearly, some outraged marine or truculent convict. For a moment he saw Brugden's powerful shoulders, imagined his arm bent back to strike.

She showed him how the beating had opened a long cut on her arm and hurt her finger, showed him the long stick-shaped weal where blood was beading on Tugear's back. She turned her face up to him, full of pain and outrage.

He cradled her hand in his own and looked at it, bent the finger gently and watched her face. It was not broken, but it was swollen. He picked up her other hand, comparing the swollen finger with the other. He went carefully so he would not touch the injured part, but she pulled back.

'*Didyi didyi!*'

There was an accusing note to her voice, although he could not have caused her pain.

He leaned forward to have a better look at the cut on Tugear's back, but she flinched in fear. Her face was turned away.

'*Minyin barakut, Tugear, minyin?*' he said, why are you afraid, Tugear?

Without looking at him she muttered, '*Mullayin.*' Because of the men.

Tagaran pointed to the cut, as if he could not see it, or could not understand that it hurt.

'*Didyi murri!*' Something like, it is very painful!

Rooke could not stop himself thinking of that other back he had so recently seen.

Had Tagaran seen it? He thought not. But something about her manner told him that she had heard about it. He could not meet her eye.

She told him the story again, with even more dramatic gestures. Her voice was shrill with outrage.

Then she watched him.

Rooke knew what she wanted. She wanted him to ask questions: *Who did this to you? Why? Where is he now?* She wanted him to join her in indignation, to put on his jacket and stride away to the settlement to deal with the white man who had beaten them.

But there was a heavy place inside him, where the event was sitting undigested like a piece of bad food.

'*Ngia muri yurora,*' he said, I am very angry.

But he knew that he did not sound angry. What he heard in his voice was a dragging reluctance, a withholding.

'*Ngalariwa?*' Tagaran asked, with us?

'No! No, of course not with you!'

It was such a wrong idea that he looked at her in surprise.

Meeting her gaze, he saw that she had asked the question to make him look at her.

'*Kamara ngyini piaba?*' she asked, *kamara* will you speak?

He had never thought that he might wish to understand less.

This exchange was not a language lesson. It was a conversation. For the first time, he and Tagaran were on the same side of the mirror of language, simply speaking to each other. Understanding went in both directions. Once two people shared language, they could no longer use it to hide.

'*Nganawa?*' he said. To whom?

'*Charlotte birang,*' she said, to the person belonging to *Charlotte.*

Not Brugden, then, but one of the sailors. He imagined himself being rowed out to *Charlotte,* asking to see the captain. *Sir, some man from your ship has beaten three native girls, I wish you to discover and punish him.*

The captain would look at him. *Really, Lieutenant? Native girls, eh?*

Some sailor or other would be brought up from below, would stand wooden-faced, the way they were taught. He would have the story ready about how he had gone ashore and the girls had stolen his bread, or his pipe.

He could imagine the scene, but not himself in it.

The girls were a tableau of brown limbs and angled faces and eyes watching Lieutenant Rooke trying to imagine the impossible.

'*Yenaraou bisket?*' Worogan said. May I go and fetch the biscuit that is still left?'

He thought he had managed the business of giving them biscuit while leaving a fragment for himself, but they had not missed a single thing. Not about the biscuit. Much less about the fact that *kamara* was not going to stand up for them.

He got the piece of biscuit and tried to amuse them by grimacing and grunting, trying to break it and failing—it was rock-like, he did not have to pretend—until he picked up the hatchet from beside the fire and chopped it into three.

Worogan and Tugear were willing to be amused by his play-acting. He was waiting for Tagaran to forgive him.

As he gave her some biscuit he pointed to her finger.

'*Murra bidyul?*' he asked, hoping this might mean *finger better?*

'*Bial, karangun,*' she said, shaking her head and making a face. Not better but worse, he supposed. Still, she seemed to have accepted that sympathy was as far as he was going to go.

When they had finished their morsels of biscuit, she made a great show of playing hostess, introducing the others to various mysteries of the hut that were new to them. She demonstrated how you made a spark with the flint, showed them how you sharpened the hatchet with the whetstone, she opened the box to show them the sextant. She wagged her finger in warning not to touch and pointed up. As she herself had done the first day, the two girls looked at the shingles, and he watched her give out a stream of words the meaning of which he was pretty sure was close to, *No, silly, not the roof, the stars!*

There were few enough objects in the hut for him to be aware of her avoiding the one in the corner behind the door: his musket. In the absence of enough pegs and shelves, its muzzle had made a convenient spot for him to hook small items of clothing. Most of the time he could forget that it was a weapon, but now he was aware of it there, and of Tagaran ignoring it.

Then Tugear said something and they were off, suddenly, like a flock of those chattering birds that came down to the grass and then all took fright at once.

He watched them clambering up the rocks. Near the top they turned and waved.

'Goodbye! Goodbye! Goodbye!'

How they seemed to love the sound of that word.

He waved until they had disappeared over the crest of the ridge, and even then went on standing there, looking up.

When he went into the hut he could no longer avoid a glum awareness of failure. What Tagaran had wanted was impossible. He tried it in his mind again: going out to *Charlotte*, knocking on the door of the captain's cabin, the man looking at him. *Native girls, you say?*

Impossible.

He thought that Tagaran knew all along that it was a test he would fail, and she had forgiven him. It only confirmed something that she understood already. In this, as in so many things, she was ahead of him.

They all knew what he had turned his face away from: like it or not, he was *Berewalgal*. He wore the red coat. He carried the musket when he was told to. He stood by while a man was flogged. He would not confront a white man who had beaten his friends.

He had been pretending that it was not so. A world existed here in his hut, a world he shared with Tagaran and the others. It was on another orbit altogether from the one he shared with his own kind. But a man could not travel along two different paths. Tagaran knew that. Now he knew it too.

The gloom that had fallen over his day was a fact he had until now denied: that the pleasure he found with Tagaran cast a shadow. He had been brushed by its wing this afternoon, just a touch. It would return. What he shared with Tagaran was the greatest delight he had ever known. But bound up with the delight, inseparable from it, was a universe of impossibility.

*

There was this about Sydney Cove, Rooke thought: at
the end of every summer's day the nor-easter came
through, as dependably as if someone out in the
endless waters of the Pacific Ocean were paid to open a window.
The forest-covered promontories seethed under gusts of wind
that darkened the water to gunmetal grey.

Rooke considered destroying the notebooks. He would
make a copy that would omit any entries which could be misun-
derstood and burn the originals. He got as far as sitting at the
table and opening a new notebook, but could not make himself
go on. To read the entries with an eye for what could be distorted
would be to distort them. He would enter that coarse way of
looking and be dirtied by it. Making an expurgated version
of the notebooks would kill them. Like a stuffed parrot, they

would be real, but not true.

When he saw Barringan threading her way down the rocks, Boneda calling *kamara, kamara,* and Tagaran a shining figure in the sun, he was glad. But he was also aware of something else in his heart. Could you want something, and dread it at the same time? Some powerful conflict of feelings in the vicinity of his chest made him unable to return her greeting.

Today it seemed the children did not want to crowd into the hut. Tagaran went in, though, and as he followed her he could not stop himself looking up at the ridge, dreading to see Silk's dapper figure.

Tagaran went straight to the corner, removed the handkerchief draped over the end of the musket, and picked it up. He put out a hand to stop her, but she had already got it snugged into her shoulder and her finger was already against the trigger. Now she was pretending that she knew how to squint along its length.

Where had she seen that done? And why had she waited till now to try the thing?

The memory of that first day on the beach came into his mind, clear as an engraving in a frame: Weymark demonstrating the power of the white man's weapon and himself laughing at the surgeon's blunt description of what a musket ball might do to a man. Rooke had not really been amused. He wondered now what had possessed him to laugh.

News of that display would have travelled from tribe to

tribe. Tagaran had most likely heard of it. Was she thinking of that picture too?

He smiled in a discouraging way, took the gun from her, put it back in the corner.

But she picked it up again and stuck her finger in the end of the barrel. She was asking, *What makes the shot come out?*

The governor had given orders that the marines never let the natives see that it was necessary to put anything into the gun. 'They must think it is the thing itself, that its effect is as immediate and simple as that of their own lances,' he had said. 'For the safety of all of us, do not let them see the loading of it.'

So Rooke shook his head, held up his thumb and asked her what it was called. She was not to be distracted. Her insistence today seemed different from her usual curiosity, when she might want to know how the lid came off the inkwell or what the buckle on a shoe was for.

Or did it only seem different, because of that new shadow over things?

Finally, because he found it so hard to refuse her, he thought to go halfway. Against both his orders and his own dragging reluctance, he got down the bag of shot and emptied a ball out into his palm. She snatched it up, felt it, weighed it and tried it with her teeth before giving it back. Rooke loaded it into the muzzle, wadded it down.

He watched her face, intent on the movement of the ramrod in and out. He could see that she had forgotten that he was *kamara.* For the moment he was nothing more than a conduit for the knowledge she wanted.

His hands knew the movements of this ritual so well he could have loaded the gun with his eyes closed. In Portsmouth they had drilled endlessly, the sergeant calling out the actions one by one. It was incredible to Rooke now, but he had seen in the gun only a marvel of logic and mechanics.

On Tagaran's face he saw an echo of that fascination, and wanted to say, *There is nothing to admire here.*

He hoped the palaver of loading and wadding the shot would be enough, but Tagaran was not fooled. She pointed to the pan, the duckbill hammer, the flint, demanded to see what they all did, so he showed her how the hammer struck the flint and made a spark. But still she knew there was more, and that it lived in the little bag up on the shelf.

With ceremony and much appearance of care, he opened the bag and shook out a little powder into his palm. He put the pinch of powder on the pan, but did not do the essential thing; there was no powder behind the shot to spit it out along the muzzle.

At least in the letter of the law, he was still on the right side of obedience.

She followed him outside. He expected the women to be there sitting as usual around their fire, Boneda and the other children running about the rocks and up and down from the water, but for once they were nowhere to be seen.

'Where is Mauberry, where is Boneda?' he asked Tagaran, but she was not interested in the question, only in seeing what he would do next with the gun.

There was something a little odd, a little unsettling, about the emptiness of the place. Lucky, though, he supposed. The noise he was about to make would have frightened the babies.

Tagaran wanted to stand next to his shoulder, but he made her go back a few yards. She watched, huge-eyed, as he pretended to aim and pulled his finger against the trigger. The flint fell against the steel, the spark fell onto the gunpowder in the pan. She jumped back at the bright flash and screamed, but it was more delight than fear.

He could feel his face stiff around the feelings the sound awoke in him.

'There,' he said, swinging the gun down from his shoulder and standing it butt-up on the ground. 'I have shown you every-thing, does that make you content?'

But she had not been taken in. She knew he had made noise and light, but that the shot was still in the barrel.

Just for this day, he could have wished her stupid.

With gestures that an imbecile could not have mistaken, she showed him what she wanted: to see the lead ball—she picked up another one to demonstrate—hurtle itself out of the muzzle.

He would not. The noise and the flash were part of the allure of the machine, like fireworks or a person getting a note out of a tuba. But to shoot a piece of metal out of it that could penetrate a shield or a human body and expose the shambles within: that was of another order of experience, another language. What it said was, *I can kill you.*

He did not want her to learn that language. Certainly not from him.

'No. I will not. *Bial. Bial.*'

She pouted and cajoled and wheedled. Then she turned to the sulks and called him *tamunalang*, one who refuses, or, he supposed, a churl.

He thought at first it must be a game: *Tagaran gets her own way.* But still she insisted, grabbing the barrel of the gun and pushing it at him. He was sickened by it: this innocent wanting to play at death.

He thought she must see his misery at handling the gun, at being reminded that he was a soldier, his profession violence. Why did she insist?

'No! Do not ask, I beg you!'

For this appeal he had no *Cadigal* words. He had never before had to entreat her.

He snatched the thing away from her and put it behind him, out of her reach, then took hold of her wrist to stop her taking it again. Her arm was as thin as a twig, but strong. He could feel the sinewy power of it.

'Come, girl,' he cried at last. 'Do not insist! I have said no!'

He could hear the anger in his voice, and she heard it too. She answered it with a flow of vehement words, spitting them out at him. He let her go and she took a step back. They watched each other. Suddenly it was no game.

He was bewildered. He had never thought to use his strength against her, or to speak to her in anger.

He watched her face, tightened against him, half hidden by her hair, her chin obstinate. He did not understand what had happened, except that it had to do with the wretched gun. He might as well have let it off. Something had been bent out of shape by his anger as surely as it would have been by shooting.

She turned away towards the door. He took a step after her.

'Tomorrow,' he said to her back. '*Parribugo*. Will you come again tomorrow?'

She spoke without looking at him.

'*Kamara*, goodbye.'

What a terrible word that was. He could not say it in return. It was a word like a knife.

'*Parribugo*. I will be here. *Parribugo!*'

But she had gone. He watched her climb up the track, her long skinny legs moving tirelessly over the rocks. He was waiting for her to turn around. He would wave for her to come back. He would run up the track to join her.

But she did not turn.

∗

225

When she had gone, Rooke sat down on the side of his bed. His legs were trembling and he could feel an obstacle in his throat, as if part of him were trying to get out.

The smell of gunpowder still hung in the air from the pinch he had exploded for her. The smell made him feel panicked and muddled.

Why did Tagaran want to know how to fire a gun?

He found his mind suggesting an answer. How would it be—just to speculate—if Tagaran had been chosen by the natives to learn the language of the great-distance-off-people? To learn their ways? Even, perhaps, to make sense of the marks on paper that were so significant to them? To understand all their private inner workings of intellect, custom, belief and feeling?

And, perhaps, to find out how the guns worked. Their powers, their limitations. How they might be countered by men with spears and wooden shields.

A clever child like Tagaran was the perfect choice: quick to learn, but innocent. Curious, full of questions, but only a child. He thought of the way she absorbed words on a single hearing, made sense of entire sentences with amazing speed. She had learned more than she had ever taught him.

He had begun by thinking of Tagaran as a resource. He thought he had appointed her his teacher. He had been made too confident by his own ambition.

Brutally, he made himself face the last thought: he had been flattered by her friendship.

Now, to put it plain, it seemed that he was the one who had been used.

It hurt to have been taken for a fool. But that was not the pain in his throat, the constricted feeling, as if he were no longer sure how to breathe. The hurt that was choking him was that she had not enjoyed his company, after all. She had valued him only for what he could give her.

Which was how he had begun by thinking of her. Until now, when it was perhaps too late.

*

The next day, after the noon readings, Rooke set off up the track. At the top of the ridge he did not go down towards the settlement but in the opposite direction, towards the bay on the other side, the one called Long Cove. He had often seen the smoke rising there, and Tagaran had told him how the cockles and thick mud oysters loved the still water of that narrow bay. Once he had gone with her as far as a big rock from which the camp could be seen: a couple of bark shelters, a patch of cleared earth, a fire. She had made it clear that he should not go further, and he had not insisted. He had thought there would be other days, other opportunities.

Standing beside that rock today he could see that the cove was empty. No smoke rose from the mound of coals on the cleared space. The huts were still there, but empty.

He felt a hollowness within, as if he had mislaid something and might not find it again.

He sat down on the rock that was the boundary between his world and Tagaran's. The sun had already left the deep fold of the cove. The water was black, the mangroves sombre, merging with their reflected copies.

The ridge on the other side of the cove was about to hide the sun. The earth was rolling on, carrying with it the speck of life that was Daniel Rooke. Whatever took place down here among the rocks and the trees, where human beings stumbled through their days in confusion of spirit, the earth continued to spin on itself and to draw its gigantic ellipse. Its urge to fly out into space was precisely balanced by the inward pull of the sun. Whether an individual could see it or not, the sun was always blazing, always pulling, and the earth was always held by its mighty hand.

The water shifted, two ducks crossed from one point to another. Somewhere on the far bank, a bird was making the same sound over and over—whik! whik! whik!—as steadily as a man counting sheep through a gate. Out in the centre of the dark bay, a circular ripple formed that multiplied out and out, ring after perfect ring.

All this was nothing but surface for him: surface without meaning. He could hear the bird, see the ripple. That was all. It was no further than a dog might understand.

In Portsmouth he knew—so well he had forgotten ever

learning it—that when the leaves of the plane trees became yellow and leathery it meant that the weather would soon be cold. When the moon was ringed with a luminous pearliness, the next day the sea would be hurling broken water against the shingle. The fact of the leaves or the moon connected to other facts, each linked in the vast web of nature's logic.

In New South Wales, he could not see how things were connected to any larger meaning. It gave life here an oddly disjointed and tiring aspect, like moving through the world blind.

Tagaran knew the inner ligatures of this place in the way he knew those of Portsmouth. She would be blind there, he supposed, as he was here.

She had asked him one day to tell her about the place he was from.

'A harbour, like this one,' he said, and pointed to show her.

He had looked across the water towards the land of the *Cammeragal* and could see it as Portsmouth Harbour, looking over to Gosport.

'A little way across from shore to shore, like this.'

She had listened solemnly and looked where he was pointing.

He remembered the boy he had been at her age, and all the afternoons he had spent on the stony beach under the Tower, chilled through and through but dreading the return to the Academy. That boy had dreamed of beginning all over again, of a place where things could start from zero, not haunted by all those earlier failures. To be without words had been part of that dream. Now, on this wild point of land in this most distant of continents, that childish longing had come to pass. He had marvelled at it, a miraculous naked rebirth.

'A good place,' he told her.

Why had he said that, when it was not true? When you only had a few words to exchange, that was what happened. Truth needed hundreds of words, or none.

She had nodded. She thought she understood, but how could she? He had not tried to explain how it had really been, how it was to be lonely among your own people.

What was it like to be Tagaran? To walk about the woods barefoot and naked, as easy as he had been on Church Street?

He looked over his shoulder but he was alone on the hillside. The urge was irresistible, like hunger or thirst: to unbuckle his shoes, peel off the worn stockings, and stand barefoot on Tagaran's earth. His feet were as white as those fat caterpillars that were found here among rotting wood: vulnerable, weak-looking. He took a few wary steps along the track, then he was jabbed in the heel by something sharp enough to make him gasp. When he looked he saw it was only a piece of twig half the size of a toothpick. Was that how little it took to prevent him from walking in Tagaran's feet?

All his life he had liked his own company better than anyone else's. But now he was full of unease, like being too hot or too cold, or hungry or thirsty. It was none of those. It was that he was no longer sufficient to himself. There was one human, of all the humans on this spinning globe, whose company he longed for.

That was an education for a man who thought he knew most things.

He had been foolish, standing on his dignity as a soldier of His Majesty. He should simply have shot the damned thing off, and let her learn from it whatever she chose.

＊

Back at the hut he got out the notebooks that contained their conversations. They were small enough that they could be covered by his hand. Shabby and insignificant, they were the most precious things he had ever owned.

He did not expect her to return. What was recorded on these pages was all he would ever have of her.

He opened one at random. There was that first, ebullient entry: *Marray—wet*. He could remember the triumph of it. He had been so satisfied with himself, he saw now, that he had even put a full stop.

He was chilled by the confidence of those entries. How misplaced had been his triumph, how wrong the dogmatism of that full stop. *Marray*. Yes, it might have meant *wet*. It might have meant *raindrop*, or *on your hand*. It might have meant *dirty* or *mud*, because the drops on his palm had made mud out of the dust that had been there. It might have meant *pink*, the colour of that palm, or *skin*, or *braided line of love, dearie*, the way the gypsy woman at Portsea Fair had once told him.

But written down like that, with its little full stop, the possibility of doubt was erased. The meaning would never be questioned again. What had felt like science was the worst kind of guesswork, the kind that forgets it is a guess.

And, of course, he knew now that *marray* did not mean *wet*, but was an augmentive, something like *very*.

When the boy ran off, that first day, Tagaran had said *yennarrabe* and he was sure it could only mean, *He is gone*. He could see now that he had wanted to understand too quickly. He took up his pen, dipped it in the ink and turned the full stop into a comma, adding: *the English of which is not yet certain.*

He turned to the long entry which Silk had read, and relived all its awkwardness. *Goredyu tagarin, I more it (that is, I take more of it) from cold. That is to take off the cold. At this time Tagaran was standing by the fire naked, and I wished her to put on clothes, on which she said Goredyu tagarin, the full meaning of which is, I will or do remain longer naked in order to get warm sooner, as the fire is felt better without clothes than if it had to penetrate through them.*

Ingenious as this interpretation of Tagaran's words had been, it was not correct. He saw that, although *gore* was to warm, *goredyu* could very well be a different word altogether.

There was room between the lines for him to admit to his

error. *This is a mistake. Goredyu signifies something else. Gore, to warm.*

He had thought himself superior to Silk, who was innocent and smug in his belief that there was a precise unambiguous equivalence between words, and that one could exchange them as one might trade a Spanish dollar for two shillings and five pence. Now he saw that he had done the same. He had made these lists of verbs, these alphabets, these pages stretched like a net: *other inflexions of the same verb.*

But learning the Sydney tongue was not like that. Both the language and the act of learning had burst out of the boundaries he had tried to put around them. Proof of that was what he had just done. The press of the unknown had made him invent a new language, even newer to him than the *Cadigal* tongue: the language of doubt, the language that was prepared to admit *I am not sure.*

What he had not learned from Latin or Greek he was learning from the people of New South Wales. It was this: you did not learn a language without entering into a relationship with the people who spoke it with you. His friendship with Tagaran was not a list of objects, or the words for things eaten or not eaten, thrown or not thrown. It was the slow constructing of the map of a relationship.

The names of things, if you truly wanted to understand them, were as much about the spaces between the words as they were about the words themselves. Learning a language was not a matter of joining *any two points* with a line. It was a leap into the other.

To understand the movements of the celestial bodies, it was necessary to leave behind everything you thought you knew. Until you could put yourself at some point beyond your own world, looking back at it, you would never see how everything worked together.

In company with Tagaran he had glimpsed how everything found its place with everything else. He was afraid that was all he would ever have: a glimpse.

PART FOUR

To Be of the Party

*

Then Brugden crept into the settlement with a foot and a half of spear sticking out of the side of his chest. Rooke heard of it when the boy from the regiment arrived gasping at his hut.

'They got the gamekeeper, sir. He is done for.'

He could hardly speak for panting, but there was excitement in him too, the idea of being *done for* nothing more than words for this red-faced boy, the blood vivid in his cheeks.

Rooke received the news numbly. The only surprise was his lack of surprise. The emptiness he felt within himself, the gap where happiness had once been, was made concrete by this news. A bewitched time, an impossible time, had come to an end for his private self. Of course it should come to an end in a public way as well.

'Major Wyatt says.' The boy screwed his eyes up tight to get the message right. 'He says will Lieutenant Rooke kindly attend at the barracks this evening at six o'clock, sir, with his compliments, that is.'

Rooke thought, I can feign illness, can tell the boy that *Lieutenant Rooke sends his compliments but is indisposed.*

But Major Wyatt was nobody's fool.

'Sir, to regard this as an order, he says,' the boy went on, 'and Lieutenant Rooke to consider himself under obligation to be present…' The boy gaped, trying to remember the major's words. 'No matter what, sir, was the gist of it.'

*

The news had gone around the settlement like a dark flood and in the barracks the mood was ugly. Brugden had been allowed the authority that belonged to a soldier even though he was not even a free man. No one around the table had liked that, or liked the man himself. But everyone knew that nothing could be the same now, because Brugden was the governor's own man.

Silk was the centre of attention. It seemed that he was already master of the story.

'The gamekeepers went to the place near Botany Bay that they call Kangaroo Ground,' he said. 'They saw some natives creeping towards them with spears in their hands and the others were alarmed. "Don't be afraid," Brugden said, "I know them.""

The room was silent, every man watching Silk as if seeing the picture he was so vividly drawing. But, Rooke thought, how did Silk know it had been like that?

'He laid down his gun and spoke to them in their own tongue, of which he evidently knew a few words, as some of us do. But one of them jumped on a fallen tree and, without the least warning, launched his spear, which lodged in Brugden's side. Where it remains.'

He looked around as if expecting applause.

'And…' Willstead did not quite know what words to use.

'Oh he lives yet. The weapon penetrated his ribs but did not kill him outright.'

There was a stirring around the table, relief or anticlimax, was there even disappointment? Violence had an enlivening effect. As long as someone else was the victim it made the blood pump, gave the world an edge of glamour.

Rooke was surprised at the harshness of his judgment.

Silk had not finished.

'Yes, he lives still.'

His voice was almost casual, so the men had to lean forward.

'He will die, of course. But only by inches.'

'That poor devil,' Timpson murmured to Rooke. 'It could have been you or me, Rooke. Mark my words, there will be no going back from this.'

But Silk raised his voice over the hubbub.

'One of the natives was brought to the hospital. He told us that, if any attempt were made to extract the spear, death would instantly follow.'

A silence fell around the table. Rooke felt a dragging within him, deep and private and inescapable, the way he imagined the spear inside Brugden. You would long to rip it out. That would be the worst, knowing that you could not. You would die with it next to your heart, an enemy closer than any lover.

Gamekeeper. He wondered whether that word had killed Brugden.

'Warungin examined the spear,' Silk continued, 'and without the slightest hesitation pronounced the assailant to be one Carangaray, of the Botany Bay tribe.'

Rooke had heard Warungin speak of Carangaray. The man might even have been one of those who arrived now and then at Rooke's hut, to be entertained by Warungin's mimicry of Major Wyatt.

The anger in the room was like a draught against Rooke's skin or a smell in the air. He shrank into his corner at the end of the long table. He wished he were in his hut, the candle casting its friendly light, wished it yesterday, wished Brugden swaggering about as before, with no spear between his ribs.

Something had ended and something else was beginning.

He wanted nothing to end, nothing to begin.

'The gun is the only language the buggers will understand,' Lennox said. 'Mark my words, a few deaths and we would be shot of them for good. Forget all that flummery about amity and kindness.'

At the head of the table, Major Wyatt gazed into space, hearing nothing.

Silk took it on himself to be the diplomat. 'As we speak, His Excellency is considering the best course of action,' he said. 'He went so far as to condescend to ask my opinion of various alternatives. I assure you, gentlemen, he has it well in hand, and will act in the interests of every one of us.'

Rooke caught the eye of Willstead, sitting opposite, who rolled his eyes.

'But when, that is the question,' he muttered to Rooke behind his hand. 'How long will they go unpunished, how long before the governor does what he should have done months ago?'

Major Wyatt decided to acknowledge this and thundered from the end of the table. 'Lieutenant Willstead, I will thank you to have a care, if you please, let us hear no more of this!'

Lennox had continued to think about what a musket might do. 'Simple enough matter to round up some of the ones here among us,' he said. 'Make an example. Would soon get back to the rest. They are all in league with each other, you know.'

'They none of them can be trusted,' Willstead said. 'They

have never been known to attack in fair fight. They lurk and they skulk and they smile, and attack a man only when he is unarmed. I believe, in fact, that they do not even have a word for treachery in their vocabulary.'

On the word *vocabulary* Silk glanced down the table at Rooke, but said nothing.

Rooke had no idea whether the natives had a word for treachery. His conversations with Tagaran had never travelled in that direction.

Even in English, treachery was a word with a broader reach than it was entitled to. What it boiled down to was that the men in this hut had been taught to fight by certain rules. Not fighting in accordance with those rules was treachery.

There might be another way of looking at what the natives did, Rooke thought. He imagined Warungin explaining. Uninvited guests had arrived in his home. They had been pleasant, offered small gifts. But then they had stayed, longer than visitors should, and rearranged the place to suit themselves.

His grandmother had had a saying for it. *There are two things that stink after three days,* she would say. *Fish and visitors.*

*

Late the next day Rooke heard footsteps outside. He leaped up from the table, in his haste knocking over the chair. He almost fell across the room to the doorway. But it was not Tagaran.

For once Silk was grave-faced. He came into the hut, taking a seat in front of the fire without waiting to be asked.

'Well, Rooke,' he said. 'It seems that we are to be sent out on a task of considerable significance.'

Rooke busied himself filling their cups with sweet-tea.

Silk answered the question Rooke had not asked. 'To Botany Bay,' he said. 'Where they got Brugden. The governor summoned me this afternoon. A punitive expedition is to be mounted, which I have the honour of leading.'

Rooke saw a shine in his eye and something about the corners of his mouth that was at odds with his solemn manner.

'Well done,' Rooke said, and raised his cup.

'Thank you, Rooke! It is gratifying, I own, to have the governor's notice in this matter.'

'Carangaray. That is the name, I think. Of the man?'

Rooke's voice was flat but he noticed with interest that his heart was beating fast. Silk took the raised cup as a toast, clinked his own against Rooke's.

'Carangaray is indeed the name, and my instructions are simple. We are to bring in six of those natives who reside near the head of Botany Bay.'

'Six of the natives? Not Carangaray alone?'

'Actually, Rooke, between you and me, the governor had wished to bring in ten men. I suggested that six would serve the purpose as well, and he was kind enough to agree with my view.'

'Ten men,' Rooke said. 'I see.'

But Silk was not concerned with arithmetic.

'When the governor asked which men I wished to make up the party, naturally yours was the first name I mentioned. You and Willstead and myself. Two days, thirty privates, double rations.'

Rooke smoothed with a finger at his cup, where a crack made a line down one side. He tried to picture it: the string of men walking through the woods, thirty men and the officers, double rations bouncing along in the packs on their backs, a musket hanging from its strap over every man's shoulder.

He could see the picture, could hear the clanking of their kettles as they marched, the snapping of the twigs. But he could not see himself. Could not put himself in that line of men, the compass in his hand, the gun over his own shoulder.

Being reminded that he was a soldier, a man who had sworn to serve and obey, was like forcing open a rusted hinge.

'No,' he said without thinking. Once uttered, it seemed right. 'I think not. No.'

The wind flung itself in spurts against the hut, rattling the flap of the door, making the canvas of the observatory dome thrum and snap.

Silk fingered the whitewashed planks of the wall beside his shoulder. A speck of white drifted down, passing brilliantly, as if showing off, through a beam of sunset that streamed in where the mud between the planks had fallen away.

It was as if he had not heard Rooke speak.

'The governor asked me, which officers would I take? I named them. Rooke and Willstead.'

He licked his finger and used the spit to glue back some loose flakes of whitewash.

'See? He has your name, Rooke.'

The stripe of sun fell on his scarlet shoulder, putting his face in shadow.

'I think no is not an answer.'

Thirty men walking through the woods, each man watching his feet and the back of the man in front. And behind trees and in the high places of rocks, the natives watching. Seeing *kamara*, friend of Tagaran, a person in whose mouth their language was beginning to take shape, marching with the others, his musket over his shoulder.

He could not think of the words that would turn Silk away.

'Do you know, Silk,' he exclaimed, hearing his voice a little wild, 'I have found that they use the dual plural, like Greek. Dual pronouns too, I think, though am not sure, but have collected some examples... *You and me*, or *all of us*, or *me and these others but not you*, all embedded in the pronoun! While English makes only the crudest of distinctions! Imagine, Silk, a race of people using a language as supple as that of Sophocles and Homer!'

He was going to go on, his voice louder now with excitement, his hands drawing pictures on the air of *you and me*, of *all of us*, of *me and these others but not you*.

'Rooke, I am beside myself with fascination,' Silk said. 'But Sophocles and Homer are not to the point. The point being, I have given your name to the governor. He has your name and he knows you to be the best man for getting us there and back without losing our way. Now there's a good fellow, we leave on Wednesday, and will be gone two days, and there will be no more of this business of spearing our men as they go about their business in the woods.'

There was a long silence. The beam of sun had moved, or perhaps it was Silk's shoulder.

Rooke watched his foot, moving the toe of his worn old shoe into the sun, out of the sun. He could not say to Silk, *I cannot do this, because the men we bring in might be the uncles, the cousins, even the brothers of Tagaran.* Could not say, *I cannot do this, because I am too fond of Tagaran.*

Fond? he imagined Silk repeating. *Too fond of a native girl to obey an order?*

'Do not ask me,' Rooke said. 'As you are a friend, do not ask me. I would not deny you, only do not ask. I have friends here among the natives. As you know.'

Silk cleared his throat.

'Yes. I am, shall we say, aware. But Rooke, think: this is not a request, it is an order.'

Rooke watched dust puff and subside in the shaft of sunlight. Dust seemed weightless, until you watched it fall.

'You know as well as I do, Rooke, the way they hide in the

woods. We know how clever they are at hiding. When have we ever succeeded in finding natives who did not want to be found?'

His face was warm, coaxing.

Silk was right. They watched from behind trees and rocks, their skins part of the speckled light and shade of the place. From half a mile away they would hear the passage of thirty men through the woods, sixty feet crushing leaves and twigs underfoot, sixty hands pushing bushes aside, thirty kettles clanking on thirty packs. Not to mention the officers. Another three packs, another six shoes. Two of them belonging to himself.

'Rooke, old fellow,' Silk said, 'You know the governor cannot let the spearing of that poor wretch go unremarked. His own gamekeeper, a terrible lingering death ahead of the poor devil. A show of force is required. Thirty armed men: would he be ordering a force of that size to take a handful of natives? You could think of it as a piece of theatre, Rooke, if you wished.'

Rooke could imagine Warungin in his gregarious mood, telling the story of how the white men had blundered through the woods while he watched from behind a tree.

'I know you are a man of principle, my friend, and I respect you for it,' Silk said. 'Your scruples do you credit. But this is a simple enough thing, two days on the march and then life will resume as before.'

He did not wait for Rooke to say yes. 'We leave on

Wednesday, at sunrise. I will send the lad out with your rations and so on.'

Silk was too quick, Rooke thought. He had run along the broad road of his argument and arrived at the end, panting and pleased, while Rooke was at a standstill, trying to remember how to put one foot in front of the other.

Silk reached for his hand, shook it.

'Good man, Rooke. Until Wednesday!'

And was gone.

＊

It was time for the evening reading of the instruments. Mechanically Rooke went through the motions. He walked between each instrument and the ledger, dipping the pen in the ink, putting the number where it belonged. *Wind, S-S-W, 3 knots. Weather, fine. Remarks: none.*

He wished Gardiner were here. His absence was like a cold wound. He was the only man whose advice he would trust. What would Gardiner say?

He remembered the grim way Gardiner had agreed that they were all loyal subjects of the Crown. He had never again referred to the duty that was *by far the most unpleasant he ever had to execute.*

Gardiner would spell out the consequences of refusal. Rooke had done the same for him: remind him that the service of humanity and the service of His Majesty were not congruent.

It had been simple enough to speak to Gardiner of duty. It must have sounded glib, he thought now. He wished he could tell Gardiner, *I am sorry, my friend, I spoke too easily.*

Until this point in his life he had allowed himself to be propelled by circumstance, situation, need. He had never had to take the grain of life in his bare hands and twist it to another shape. Never stopped and asked, *But what am I doing?*

Silk's logic seemed unassailable: the expedition would fail, and so there was no reason to refuse it. But if the governor were merely performing a piece of theatre in the interests of intimidation, where was the fearsomeness, what was the deterrent, if the terrific procession met not a single native because they were all laughing from behind bushes as it passed?

'The logic is faulty, you see.'

He was startled to find he had spoken aloud.

Still, the central fact remained: the expedition would fail. Whether or not the governor hoped to capture six natives and whether or not Silk hoped the same, it was almost certain that no native would be caught.

Almost.

'It could be done, however,' he said. He could see how a man might get into the habit of talking to himself. It cleared the mind, to hear the words aloud, as if spoken by a sympathetic other who knew you as well as you knew yourself.

'I could do it.'

R ooke could have gone looking for Warungin or
Boinbar, but that would have meant allowing himself
to know what he was doing. Instead he set off towards
the settlement as if on some errand. He watched his feet on the
uneven ground and did not think beyond one step, another
step.

He left the thing to chance, and chance gave him the boy
Boneda, sitting by the track on a rock. He could not have been
waiting for Rooke, but showed no surprise at seeing him. He
held out the thing in his fist: a fat lizard, not quite dead. In a
stream of words and gestures Rooke only partly followed,
Boneda said something to the effect of, *I caught it over there, it ran
very fast, I am going to eat it and it will be very good.*

There was something that the eyes of the natives did when

they smiled, a gleam under their heavy brows, so that the smile seemed to come from within as much as from the play of muscles on the face.

'I want to see Tagaran.'

It sounded very blunt, like that, but it had to be clear, and he trusted Boneda's English more than his own *Cadigal*.

'Will she come to visit me? Will she come to my hut? Will you tell her, *kamara* wants to see her?'

Boneda said something Rooke could not follow, pointed in a generally west direction with his stick, and was gone, springing up the rocks towards the ridge.

Had he understood? Rooke did not know. He turned and made his way back to the hut.

He lit his fire, just a few sticks smoking away together. That was to say, *I am at home and would welcome a visitor.*

Then he lay on his stretcher, hands under his head, staring up at the shingles without seeing them.

He did not sleep, but had submerged into a stupor when there was a shadow in the doorway. Tagaran was there, hesitating. He swung his legs down and sat on the side of the bed. She was alone. She had never arrived alone before.

She came in and sat at his table, smoothing at the grain of the wood with a finger. She was waiting for him to speak. He was waiting for a miracle that would free him from the thing that had fallen on him like a great heavy cloak.

He got up and sat at the table opposite her.

'Why?' he asked in English. 'Why did the black man wound the white man?'

Her face, wary, lifted to his.

'*Gulara*,' she said, just that word. Angry.

'*Minyin gulara eora?*' Rooke asked, Why are the black men angry?

He knew the answer, but needed the words. Needed the thing they were used to, the question and the answer.

'*Inyam ngalawi white men.*' Because the white men are settled here.

He thought perhaps she needed it too, backwards and forwards, word and word.

One long hand smoothed down her forearm from elbow to wrist as if she were cold. He saw a line of pink dots that marked the graze she had received from *the person from Charlotte.*

She was looking down again. He could not see her face, only the tip of her nose and her hair.

'*Tyerun Cadigal*,' she said without looking up. The *Cadigal* are afraid.

Her fingers smoothed at the mahogany as if she could rub away the surface and see something else beneath it.

'The musket,' he began. 'Remember. You asked me, you wished, to learn. To make it shoot. To load it and shoot it.'

She went on rubbing at the polished wood, but he knew she was listening.

'Why, Tagaran? Why did you wish to know? Will you tell me?'

He heard the water slapping fretfully against the rocks at the foot of the promontory. A loose shingle rattled, the canvas of the dome creaked, a gull gave a long rueful cry. He might wait all day and hear other things, but he saw that he would not hear an answer.

He went back a step.

'*Minyin tyerun Cadigal?*' he asked, why are the *Cadigal* afraid?

'*Gunin.*' She looked him straight in the eye. Because of the guns.

The word was like a gunshot in itself.

'Brugden,' he said. He would have given the poor devil his other name, but realised he did not know it. Tagaran tilted her face even further towards the table. She knew who Brugden was, and what had happened to him.

He took a breath and made himself go on. 'Brugden will die.'

Tagaran did not look at him. So far he had told her nothing she did not already know.

'They are going out after Carangaray.'

She looked up as if he had shouted. Her hand went to her mouth and her face changed shape around this piece of information.

He sketched the movement of putting a musket up to his shoulder.

'Tomorrow. *Parribugo*. For Carangaray. For others too. Six men. Six *eora*.'

He held up fingers to show her.

That was probably enough, but having come so far, there was a luxurious yielding in going all the way to the end.

'*Piabami Warunginyi?* Will you tell Warungin? I would like you to let Warungin know.'

Tagaran looked straight into his eyes. She understood, he could see that. Not just the words, but the significance of him having said them to her.

'*Piabami Warunginyi?*' he said again.

There was a pleasure in using her language for this. Each word started emphatically and dropped away, and each sentence did the same, a sequence of diminuendos. It was a language whose very cadence sounded like forgiveness.

'Botany Bay,' she said. 'For Carangaray.'

And copied his gesture, the musket up to her shoulder.

'Yes,' Rooke said. 'Tomorrow, in the morning.'

He could hear a bird above them chattering as if scolding, the dry whisper of the leaves. Everything was going on as it always had. For centuries, for millennia, the forebears of that bird had sat out there and the forebears of those leaves had whispered in that breeze. Only in here were things changed.

'I too. I am to be of the party.'

It was a relief to say the words, but did not give the satisfaction he had hoped. Like a child, he had thought that putting the thing into words would make it go away. But it was still sitting between them while outside that callous bird did not seem to realise there was nothing to sing about.

'What is to be done, Tagaran? What is to become of us?'

This was a question beyond the game of words. It was out of the reach of their grammar lessons.

She went over to the fireplace and held out her hands to the coals. He thought it was her polite way of ending their conversation. But then she turned back to him and held out her hands for his. She pressed his fingers with her own. He felt her skin warm and smooth.

'*Putuwa*,' she said, pressing and smoothing. '*Putuwa.*'

Their hands were the same temperature now.

'*Putuwa*,' he repeated.

She pressed harder, smoothing with larger gestures and he understood the word to mean the action she was performing, that is to warm one's hand by the fire and then to squeeze gently the fingers of another person. In English it required a long rigmarole of words. In England a person who warmed their hands by the fire did so in order to thrust them into their pockets and keep them warm. Tagaran was teaching him a word, and by it she was showing him a world.

Everything in his life had come down to the sensation of her fingers against his. The person he was, the history he carried within himself, every joy and grief he had ever experienced, slipped away like an irrelevant garment. He was nothing but skin, speaking to another skin, and between the skins there was no need to find any words.

A laughing jackass began to peal from somewhere up on the ridge, and as if she had heard a clock chiming, reminding her of something she must do, Tagaran let go of his fingers.

'*Yenioo, kamara*,' she said, I am going, my friend. She looked up at him and he thought he saw in her face the same thought he had: *This is the last time we will see each other.*

He groped for words and none came. He would not give a word to the bleakness he felt. Could not say it: *goodbye.*

He followed her out of the hut, watching her climb the rocks. As he hoped, at the top she turned. He raised his arm, straight up, the hand opened towards her, and she waved back. Then she turned and was gone.

In his mind he went with her, following her along the path, turning towards the camp in the next bay, watching her go down the long traverse of the hillside past the big rock that was as far into her world as he had ever gone. She would arrive in the clear place where the fire sent up its column of smoke and the women sat on the ground as if growing out of it, where the children ran and poked among the mangroves and where, when the sun went down, they all came together to eat and sleep.

The picture was so vivid in his mind that it was a shock to find himself not there but here, alone on his windy point.

Putuwa.

Just as he did, she knew that something ugly was on its way. But she had left him a word he would never forget, and the weight of trust it carried.

At the parade ground next morning, Silk was full of energy, the early hour no hindrance to his enthusiasm. He spread out a copy of *Cook's Plan of Botany Bay* on the ground and beckoned Rooke and Willstead and the sergeant to look.

'We will first proceed south-west, travelling through Kangaroo Ground and beyond. Having made a sweep there, we will turn east and, after pausing for rest and refreshment, will launch our attack. Our objective, gentlemen, is the promontory in the northern part of the bay where there is a village of the Botany Bay tribe. We will surround the village and entrap the natives.'

'Entrap the natives,' Willstead repeated. 'Yes indeed, a good plan.'

Silk looked hard at him, but Willstead's face was bland.

This plan showed a grasp of military strategy in Silk that Rooke did not know he possessed. He had thought that Silk would simply lead them about in the woods in various directions. Instead he had come up with a plan that, without Rooke's warning to Tagaran, would have had a pretty fair chance of working. Rooke had not seen the village, but had heard it described as a collection of huts, on a narrow neck of land with deep water on three sides.

He revisited Silk's words. *Think of it as a piece of theatre, if you wish!* Yet here he was, bright-eyed with his scheme, a coil of rope looped across his chest ready for tying up prisoners.

Rooke supposed that even theatre needed to be convincing.

The sergeant got the troop of men lined up and it clanked out of the settlement like a clumsy clockwork toy of many segments which would twitch its way over the floor until the spring ran down. They marched under a low grey sky, along the same track on which Brugden had made his last journey in the opposite direction.

They had been marching for some four hours when they arrived at Kangaroo Ground, a pleasant park-like grassy expanse with large trees at intervals and a graceful slope to the land. There, just beside the track, was the hut that Brugden and the others had put together for their expeditions, constructed on the native pattern, of boughs and sheets of bark. Outside they had built a fireplace with stones, and had drawn up logs to sit on.

They had made themselves comfortable, Rooke thought. The fireplace was full of old coals. How many nights had the prisoners and their sergeant sat here, telling each other the stories of their lives? They had carved a piece of the place out for themselves, where the governor and behind him the machinery of empire could be forgotten. As Lieutenant Rooke was out on his point, at Kangaroo Ground they were free men.

The track led up slopes and down valleys. Along low ground they skirted pools of fresh water and a few minutes later a cry went up from the men at the front, 'The sea! The sea!' and they emerged on the shore of Botany Bay. Beyond the arms of land that marked its entrance, there was the ocean, the simple geometry of the horizon.

Silk called a halt and gathered the men around him.

'The village is at the northern end of this beach, men. We will return to the pools just passed and rest there for a short time before we mount our attack.'

By the side of one of the pools the men scattered themselves in what shade they could find and opened their wallets of food. They stretched out, their heads pillowed on their packs, the sergeant snoring. The handkerchief he had laid over his face against the flies puffed up and subsided with each breath.

Rooke found an embayment among tall bushes that was like a room with walls that shifted in the breeze from the sea. He lay too, but did not sleep.

It had hardly begun, but he wished this adventure over.

He went through his workings again. Proposition one: the expedition would only capture natives who did not have any reason to avoid them. Proposition two: the natives had been given reason to avoid them. Ergo, there was no chance of any capture.

Well, he corrected himself, the chance was not zero. He could not put a number on it, but told himself he did not need to concern himself with such a remote possibility.

So why could he feel his face contracting with the effort to calculate it?

He remembered something he had not thought of for years: the way Dr Vickery had once tried to put an overawed boy at ease by likening himself to a bat. But Rooke's eagerness for night was more than an astronomer's impatience. He had only to get through another six or seven hours of daylight. Then the attack on the village would be safely behind them.

Night would fall, and he could roll himself into his blanket. He could lie watching the stars until he fell asleep in their cool light.

They rested for an hour, then set off again, back to the beach and north along the edge of the trees towards the village. At the neck of the promontory Silk stopped and whispered his last orders.

'We will fan out to block any escape. Lieutenant Rooke, you will take your men as far as you can go on the north side, and spread out into a line. Lieutenant Willstead, do the same to the south, and I will take my men up the middle. We will then advance together in a cordon, and the natives will be outflanked and trapped.'

He had his pocket watch out on his palm, opening and closing it in his excitement.

'I will give you, shall we say, ten minutes. Kindly look at your watches, and in ten minutes' time precisely, having formed a human chain, you will commence your advance in order that all groups meet simultaneously at the village.'

Rooke got out his own pocket watch and checked the time. The sun blazed white on its face. Time had no intention and no judgment. A watch had only to move tooth by tooth, jerking the wheels blindly forward. Only among humans was there always this doubt, this fear, this hope and dread and wondering all washing around together like a sea against rocks.

Rooke led his men across a tangled area of sand and rope-like strands of grass, heaped and valleyed in ways that could have been designed expressly to make progress difficult. As instructed, he arranged his men across the northern part of the neck of land in a line. Ten minutes after Silk had given the order, he waved them forward.

It was hard going, floundering through sand and grass, up and down over rocks and in between clefts and sudden hollows. But then they surmounted a rise and found themselves beside the rest of the men in a ragged line at the edge of the village.

The place was as it had been described. Nine huts, solid affairs nearly high enough to stand in, were grouped around a central space in which a fire burned cheerfully, nearby some wooden dishes, a pile of mussels, a neat stack of firewood.

Silk's strategy had been perfectly planned and executed, a manoeuvre as if from a military textbook. The only problem was that the natives had not waited to be outflanked.

The sound of men catching their breath was mocked by a bird somewhere nearby: *Too wee! Too wee!* The loop of rope across Silk's chest was uncoiling, one end trailing in the sand behind him.

'There they are,' one of the men shouted.

Even as everyone turned to look, a native was pushing a canoe off from the shore, sliding in and paddling rapidly across the estuary. Three other canoes, full of natives, had almost reached the far bank. One was already drawn up on the sand there. A group of men stood looking across at where the redcoats panted. Rooke could hear cries and shouts—of fear or mirth, he could not tell.

Silk stared across. His back was straight, his narrow shoulders held stiff. The distance was not enormous, the river no wider than the Thames at Westminster, but a distance and depth impossible for a party of armed men.

Willstead was opening his mouth to speak, but Silk was there first.

'Quick, men,' he shouted. 'They are not out of range, quick now, load and fire!'

Rooke went about it slowly, even dropped his bag of shot, but all around him he could see the eagerness of the men. Next to him a heavy red-faced private was breathing noisily through his nose, the air whistling in and out as he loaded and rammed.

By the time the guns were ready, the natives were too far away for any but the luckiest of shots to find a target. One by one the men fired, Rooke among them. He fixed on a patch of glittering water far from the canoe, and hoped that for once his aim was good.

The last canoe was pitching in the swell coming from the bay. Rooke watched it while around him men put away their powder horns and slung the guns back over their shoulders.

In the stern of the canoe someone turned and looked back. It was too far away to make out features, but the figure was a child's. Across the water Rooke and the child gazed at each other, the canoe bobbing up and down, the paddles glinting wet. He was piercingly reminded of Tagaran and the stricken look she had given him when he had mimed a musket to the shoulder.

Silk turned to face the men, speaking calmly, as if everything had gone exactly to plan.

'Well done, men. Well done.'

Rooke did not think anyone was fooled by this, but no one said so.

'Now form up, we will return to the place where we rested. We will make camp there and tomorrow we will continue our search to the south.'

The party moved quickly on the way back down the beach. Rooke came along behind at a leisurely pace. All at once the afternoon was benign, the breeze coming from the sea soft against his cheek.

'A native, sir, a native in the water,' one of the soldiers called. 'Out in the water, sir!'

Rooke shaded his eyes against the glare of the water and made out a speck.

'Do not look,' Silk called. 'Mr Willstead! Mr Rooke! We will continue up the shore, we will not stop here. Pass on if you please with your faces turned away.'

Willstead still squinted out at the water.

'Do not look, Willstead,' Silk said sharply. 'You are still looking, man. March on!'

But Willstead unshouldered his musket and rested it butt-down on the sand as if prepared for an argument.

'Are we not to take him, then?'

'At this distance we can neither seize him nor shoot him. Any such efforts would simply have the effect of rendering us ridiculous. We will pass by without letting him see that we have noticed. March on, quick, man!'

They turned away, but Willstead must have been looking after all.

'He is coming to us! He is coming to join us!'

Sure enough, the man was wading through the water towards them. Rooke could see his torso turning with each step and his arms out to the sides to speed his progress.

It was no longer possible to pretend.

'Halt!' Silk called. 'We will allow him to come to us.' He was sweating, his face waxy, his faded red jacket dark under the arms.

Rooke had not thought that *a piece of theatre* would look quite like this.

'Do him no harm, men,' Silk shouted. 'No harm, do you understand? He is coming to us in trust, it is no part of our intention to betray trust, only to punish.'

His voice strained to be heard over the sounds of the breeze in the trees and the water against the shore.

'But, sir,' Willstead said. 'Are not our orders to take any male natives?'

'Take, yes, but only by force, what would be the point, man, if the native invites himself to be taken? There is no message there for the others.'

'So if they run away,' Willstead said, dogged, 'if they run away we can take them, except we cannot catch them. But if they come to us we must not take them?'

The soldiers closest to him caught this and there was a stirring, perhaps even a sniggering.

The man was running up the beach towards them. They

could see the sand spurting at each step and he was close enough now that they could see the woolly hair on his face, the band around his forehead, his feet caked with fine yellow sand like a pair of slippers: Warungin, coming to meet them with every appearance of good cheer.

He caught up to them, hardly out of breath, and greeted such men as he knew. When he came to Rooke there was not a flicker of any consciousness, no hint of acknowledging a collaborator.

If Warungin did not know the purpose of their expedition, it would be normal for him to enquire what they were doing there, and Rooke was glad when he did so. Were they hunting kangaroo? he mimed. Were they fishing, or had they come for something in the trees, honey perhaps?

Silk did not commit himself on the matter of kangaroo hunting or honey gathering.

'Warungin,' he said, smiling, the effort to appear casual evident in his voice, 'Warungin, my friend, can you tell us where we would find Carangaray? Where is Carangaray?'

Warungin frowned at the name.

He gave a short speech, in the course of which he mentioned the name Carangaray frequently, each time flicking his hand in a broad gesture that started with it hanging from the wrist and finished with the palm up, facing south.

'Mr Rooke, you are by way of being the linguist among us,' Silk said. 'What is he saying?'

'He speaks too fast,' Rooke said. 'I cannot follow.'

This was so irreproachably the truth that Silk did not insist.

Silk now tried charades to convey his meaning. Walked his fingers though the air, repeating *Carangaray*. Warungin watched stolidly, copied, the fingers walking in the air, but he improved on Silk's performance, pushing his arm out as he did so to demonstrate the idea of *a long way*. Then he did a palm-under-cheek motion and a sweeping gesture across the sky to indicate the passage of the sun. The message was unmistakable: Carangaray was at such a distance that the sun would travel two or three times across the sky, and men would lay their palms under their cheeks to sleep three or four times, to reach the place where he now was.

Much too far, in other words, for thirty heavily armed but lightly provisioned soldiers to go in pursuit.

They tramped back to the pool behind the beach. Warungin made no signs of leaving them. Willstead grumbled that he was hanging about in the hope of a meal at their expense, but Rooke did not think the delights of dry crumbled bread, and a handful of shreds of salt beef, would be much of a temptation.

As the men cut ferns to sleep on and gathered wood to last their fires through the night, Warungin did in fact disappear. Rooke and Willstead paused to watch the lightness of his step as he went off down the path with his fishgig swinging backwards and forwards.

'They come and go like children,' Willstead said. 'He is a good enough fellow, I suppose, but you could never rely on any of them. When the whim takes them, off they go.'

But, by the time they had the fire going, Warungin was back, eight plump mullet hanging from his hand, strung together with a length of vine. He scraped a few flat places among the coals, briefly cooked his catch, and then broke the fish into pieces with his fingers and shared them out among the officers. Laughed to see how squeamish they were about the heads. Took them back and crunched the heads entire, indicating how good they were.

'Well,' Silk admitted after he had licked his fingers clean, 'he may be a savage but he does seem to have some idea of *quid pro quo.*'

The fire blazed up into the growing darkness. Rooke lay back on the sand with a sigh, feeling the tension ease in his shoulders. The shape of the ground pressed up against him. Through the treetops he could see Betelgeuse, very red tonight, winking in a gap between the leaves.

In the morning there would be a few more hours of pointless tramping through the forest, then they would direct their steps back towards Sydney, empty-handed but blameless.

Silk's face was swarthy with a day's beard, sunburnt and shining in the flickering light. He would come out of this well, Rooke thought. He would regale the governor with every detail of the business. The governor would think him a fine fellow, heap praise on his head, mention him in his next despatch.

The attack on the village would make a good chapter in Silk's narrative. He had orchestrated an impressive performance. The checking of the watches was a masterstroke that would add colour to the account. Silk would mask the failure of the expedition with an amusing ruefulness and self-deprecation. There might even be a hint that the failure was no accident. He would emerge as a man who had picked his way with tact and humanity among the pitfalls of the situation. At a time when feeling ran high, he had talked the governor down from ten natives to six. The final triumph of his genius would be to come back with none, and still be praised.

It was a pity Rooke could not share his own triumph with Silk. What a lively chapter it would have made in the narrative: the neat sidestepping of a difficult situation by the unexpectedly deft Lieutenant Rooke.

He sat up, hugging his knees. There would be time now, all the time in the world, all the time in a life. He would apply for another term of duty, and another beyond that. The specifics of the future were not clear, but the outline was wonderfully simple: himself in New South Wales.

He would go on talking with Tagaran and the others. He would master the language. The day he had written *I kaadianed it*, without thinking, he had taken a step on a journey he wanted never to end.

D ouble rations, and the failure to capture a single native, had made the men raucous. Beside their bonfire on the other side of the clearing they were having something of an impromptu party. Silk looked over now and then but let them go. Among the three officers there was a peaceful silence, each man gazing into the fire with his own thoughts. Warungin was half-asleep, staring glassily into the flames, his body relaxed.

The moon rose, bright enough to make the flames sallow. By its light Rooke watched Silk unbuckling his pack and groping in it, he supposed for his journal. Rooke leaned over to help him by holding the awkward flap.

'I look forward to seeing what you make of our expedition,' he began, but he had taken hold of the bottom of the bag by mistake so that the thing upended on the sand. A hatchet slipped out, its freshly honed edge gleaming in the moonlight. Bent around it were several folded canvas bags.

'Why Silk, were you planning to cut your own firewood?' Rooke said, feeling the edge on the hatchet, sharp enough to shave with. 'With thirty men to do it for you?'

In his expansive mood, after the days of anxiety, the idea of Silk with the hatchet in his hand, chopping his own kindling, seemed the funniest thing in the world. But Silk was not amused. He grabbed the hatchet out of Rooke's hand, thrust it back into the bottom of the pack, picked up the bags and tried to jam them in after it.

Willstead was watching with an expression that Rooke could not read. There was something about the hatchet, something about the bags, that Willstead knew.

'Well, Silk, out with it!' Rooke cried. 'Did you hope to bring back a couple of trophies for Dr Weymark to paint? Or add illustrations of your own to your narrative?'

The hatchet had drawn blood, black in the firelight, on the ball of his thumb.

'Not so far off the mark, Rooke,' Willstead cried. 'Trophy is very near the case!' He was vastly entertained by some idea.

Rooke saw him glance across the fire at Warungin.

'Lieutenant Willstead!' Silk exclaimed. 'I will thank you to hold your tongue!' He had at last got the pack closed again and pushed it behind him, in the shadow cast by his body.

Willstead smirked at Rooke but said no more.

It was not the hatchet, not the bags, but the set of Silk's face, half visible in the firelight, and a tone in his voice, that sent a chill into Rooke.

A breeze passed over the trees all around, a long shiver of sound like a sigh.

A peculiar kind of sum was working away in Rooke's mind: the hatchet plus the bags, multiplied by Willstead's smirk and divided by the look on Silk's face.

'Silk,' Rooke started.

His voice caught in his throat. It seemed to have closed around the words. He coughed, tried again.

'Silk, a word, might I have a word?'

He got to his feet and jerked his head towards the darkness. Silk hesitated, then got up and followed him. Out of earshot of the men around the fire, Rooke turned to him. In the dimness he could not see what sort of expression was on his friend's face.

'The hatchet, Silk,' he said. 'And the bags.'

He could hear his own voice as neutral as a man laying out the propositions of a calculus.

'May I ask for what purpose they were brought?'

'Well, Rooke, natives were by preference to be captured and brought in,' Silk said. 'But if that did not prove practicable, then my orders were that six be slain.'

'Practicable.'

'Yes, practicable.'

'And the bags?'

'The heads of the slain were to be brought back.'

'The heads of the slain,' he repeated.

It was just words, a phrase of poetry or items off a list.

'The heads, Rooke, were to be brought back in the bags provided. Having been severed with the hatchet provided. The governor's argument was that it was necessary to act harshly once, in order not to have to act harshly again. The punishment inflicted on a few would be an act of mercy to all the others.'

'You did not tell me.'

'Rooke, my friend, the thing was never going to happen. I did not mention the hatchet because it was never going to be used. Old fellow, what is the difficulty here? No natives have been captured and no heads have been…removed. Nor will they be.'

Rooke was looking back at the men around the fire. Willstead was standing, speaking to Warungin who was sitting on the ground beside him. The light picked out parts of Warungin's face as he moved: now the cheekbone gleaming in the light, now the nose, wide and flattened, now the teeth as he laughed at whatever Willstead was trying to explain with his hands. He was leaning back, his face turned up to Willstead so the firelight shone on his throat.

How could you cut off a man's head?

You would have to make sure he was dead. That would be

the first thing. Then you would need to turn him over on his front. What with the protuberance of the nose, the side of the neck would be uppermost.

Then you would take up the hatchet. The handle was short, so you would have to get in close. It would not be a matter of one neat blow. You would have to hack at the slack skin of the neck. It would tend to slide away from the blade and the jawbone would present an obstacle.

Someone would have to hold the head so the bony part of the neck could be got at.

Then there was the matter of putting the head in the bag. Someone would have to pick it up. How heavy was a head? To pick it up by the hair would probably seem easiest. Another man would have to hold the bag open.

Whoever had the job of carrying the bag back to the settlement would be followed by a cloud of maddened flies. He might tie the bag to his knapsack to start with, but its bouncing would irritate. He would find it easier to carry it. It would be heavy: he would need to swap it from hand to hand. Could he do that without thinking of what was in there: a human head, a human face? A face like this one in front of him now, laughing with an expression half sly, half amused, and the human soul behind it, with all its exquisite nuances of feeling?

Rooke heard himself gasp, he could not catch his breath, his heart was climbing up out of his mouth, agape for the air that would not come.

Over at the fire, Warungin looked at him, half rose, put out a hand. Had he seen that Lieutenant Rooke of His Majesty's Marines was the colour of lard, and was even now stumbling away into the bushes, where he was loudly, thoroughly, sick?

✳

When the spasms had passed Rooke went down the track away from the camp. The bushes seemed to have grown over the path in the night. He buffeted his way through.

Then the last bush fell away before him and he was standing on the top of the dune behind the beach alone in the great cathedral of night. Ahead of him was a wide dark flatness. The shores all around seemed to have retreated in the night. To left and right the low runs of land were nothing more than a distant uneven line, blacker against the darkness of the bay and narrow as a ribbon. Above, the sky was another darkness, the full moon luminous, a wide eye watching.

He took a few steps down the dune and sat on the sand. On the glassy water the moon was broken up into a patch of separate shifting points of sharp light, as white against the black as a magnesium flare.

The surface seemed still, and yet small waves slid up the beach, then drew back with a hiss, leaving the lace edge of a different darkness on the sand. As each withdrew, a new flow swelled in and met the outflow with a quick liquid crash and scrape. That sound was not the wave itself but the turmoil where the coming met the going.

If you looked out at the bay, the specks of moonlight sliding across it, you would have said that it was as still as the water in a cup. Yet here it was at the edge, moving up and down, in and out, never at rest.

He could see it now as he had never seen it before: one body of water encircling the globe, the continents nothing more than insignificant obstacles around which it effortlessly flowed. The land, much less the people on it, was irrelevant to this enormous breathing being.

It was divided up on the map, its parts given different names. The names were not just irrelevant but false. It was all one, every drop acting separately and yet together with all its fellows, swelling and sinking in accordance with that plate of yellow light in the sky.

A soft shawl of cloud had come from nowhere, teased out along the leading edge like carded wool. It slipped over the moon that could be seen travelling through it like a bright eye.

Of course, it was the cloud that was travelling. It was like trying to think in two languages, knowing with the evidence of your eyes that the moon was moving through the cloud, and knowing with the evidence of your education that it was the cloud moving.

His body was pale in the moonlight when he had rid it of all its coverings. It seemed in some way another man's. Under his feet the sand was cool and satiny. He was surprised to see no blood on his hands. Only, all around him, a dark halo, the smell of his own disgust.

Breaking the skin of the water and sliding beneath it was like slipping into an extension of himself. It was warm, warmer than during the day, almost the temperature of his body. It buoyed him up, lapping itself around him, making him a floating nothing, not of land, not of sea, not of this world, not of another: not Daniel Rooke who occupied the rank of second lieutenant, but a mass without a name, displacing a certain amount of Botany Bay.

When he stood up in the shallows, he heard the water sluice off his body. He rubbed at his hands, his face, his hair. Snorted the salt up into his nostrils and out again, rinsed and spat, rinsed and spat, until the salt was stinging, his eyes flooding.

He looked back at the dense blackness of the land. He could not see the fires of the expedition from here, but could glimpse their glow, the light on the underside of the trees. He watched a mass of sparks fly up as some invisible hand threw on more wood. He heard the clink of pannikin against kettle, a sneeze, a burst of laughter.

A swell flowed in from the bay, encircling his ankles as if reminding him it was there.

He waded out of the water, walked up the beach, sat down and smoothed his hands over a patch of sand, feeling its silky coolness, the last flicker of warmth on its surface. The moon was bright, but he could see Sirius, that gem of the summer sky.

The natives would have a name for Sirius. For them it would not be part of the Great Dog. They would have some other story altogether. But whatever you called the stars, their light and their patterns were the same. Beyond the chatter of human argument was their plain statement: *Every thing is part of every other thing, now and forever.* There was no debating with them. Logic was irrelevant to them. They were blissfully indifferent to the dilemmas faced by Lieutenant Daniel Rooke, that speck of consciousness. By the timeless light of the heavens, his flicker of life meant no more than one of those sparks that flew up from the fire.

The stars could always be found where the *Almanac* put them. About the heavens, it was simple: right or wrong. Down here among the workings of humans, there was no guide that could be relied on for an answer.

Rooke had accused the governor of faulty logic. He had scoffed at Silk for it too. But he had used the same sophistry. He had persuaded himself that, as long as the expedition failed, there was no harm in being part of it.

He thought he had been so clever in warning Tagaran. He had cranked the handle of his stratagem, had smirked to see the gears mesh, the wheels begin to turn in the machine that would let him obey while keeping his hands clean.

What he could see now was that he was exactly as guilty as

the governor and as Silk. Like them, he had allowed self-interest to blind him.

He heard himself groan, a heavy inarticulate *Oh*.

It was the simplest thing in the world. If an action was wrong, it did not matter whether it succeeded or not, or how many clever steps you took to make sure it failed. If you were part of such an act, you were part of its wrong. You did not have to take up the hatchet or even to walk along with the expedition.

If you were part of that machine, you were part of its evil.

Directly ahead was the gap in the land beyond which was the ocean that had brought the *Berewalgal* two years before. He had stared from *Sirius* at the land approaching and seen nothing but opportunity. At Sydney Cove he had watched those natives running along the shore, keeping pace with the boat, shouting their unambiguous message. They had been nothing more than naked strangers. Sitting in the bow of the cutter he had had a musket ready loaded in his hands, primed to use it if ordered.

That Daniel Rooke seemed to have been replaced, syllable by syllable, by some other man. He knew those naked people now. He did not understand them, but he could no longer think of them as strangers.

A few miles to the north, beyond the woods through which a column of men had marched earlier that day, Tagaran would be lying by a fire, asleep. There would be no candle there to keep her awake, no blanket to scratch her skin. Only the night, wrapping itself around her as it wrapped itself around him. Only the moon, looking down on her as it looked down on him.

There was no word for what he had learned with Tagaran. He could not attach a name to what he felt for her. But she had shown him the existence of the man he could be.

That man was not just a lieutenant in His Majesty's service. That man knew how to sit as well as act, how to listen as well as speak, and how to feel as well as think. He had discovered truths, powerful in spite of having no names, about two people and what they might share.

That man had nothing to do with expeditions involving coils of rope and muskets, much less with sharpened hatchets and bags the right size for carrying human heads.

To remain with the expedition was to turn his back on the man he had become. But to refuse any further part in it would be to step into the void.

He could still feel the harsh sunlight of English Harbour, see the cropped heads and flapping jackets of those other lieutenants. Could still smell the shit of the one who had been hanged, still choke along with him on the rope around his throat.

Some things went too deep for forgetting.

Rooke watched the uncoiling of the water, in and out. As each wave curled over itself and fell on the sand, a gleam of light streamed along its broken edge.

It was not thought, not logic, not calculation. It was just an impulse of the body, like breathing or blinking: a reflex that was beyond reason.

'I cannot be part of this,' he said aloud.

The words left behind a windy hollow feeling that he recognised as fear. He did not know what difficult path this new Daniel Rooke might take him down, or where it would end. He knew only that he was prepared to welcome the stranger and follow where he led.

*

Back at the fire the men were rolling themselves into their blankets, arranging their handkerchiefs over their faces against the mosquitoes, banking the fire with green wood that would smoke all night.

Rooke went over to his knapsack and unfastened his blanket. The buckles seemed huge, awkward. It was his fingers, he realised. He was calm, only he could not make his fingers work.

The buckles finally forced open, the blanket unrolled, Rooke lay in it, glad of the handkerchief to hide his face. He was conscious of Silk on the other side of the fire unrolling his blanket, flapping it out with a snap, tweaking its corners straight, then lying down, folding it around him and lying still. Rooke could feel Silk listening for him to speak. *I do not know what came over me*, that was what he was expecting. *Thank you for your sound advice.*

Rooke waited until he heard steady breathing from Silk and an authoritative snoring from where Willstead lay before he set off. The moon made the sandy track plain. He would reach the settlement before dawn.

He stopped, looked back the way he had come. By moonlight both directions looked the same. Around him the bushes and trees gave off cool moist smells. Crickets pulsed, a silent black shape swooped across the sky. Something hummed close to his foot. A nocturnal insect, silent during the day? Or just such a quiet sound that it was only audible when all the other noises fell away?

He turned, hitched the knapsack further up his shoulder and walked on.

*

At dawn, as he rounded the last corner of the track before the settlement, there was the governor marching along smartly as if on his way to the brick kilns. Major Wyatt was beside him. The governor was looking at the ground and keeping up a steady stream of words while Wyatt kept his gaze respectfully on his superior's face. Then they both caught sight of Rooke and he saw on their faces the recollection, the computation.

'Lieutenant Rooke!' the governor exclaimed. 'Were you not with Captain Silk's party?'

The man was striding to meet him, almost running.

'Why are you here, where is the rest of the party?'

'Sir,' Rooke said and stopped. At some point in the night he had rehearsed what he would say to the governor. Now he was not ready, like a man with the noose about his neck being asked to say his last words and not able to think of what he had prepared.

'Sir, I.'

I eat, you eat, we eat. We have eaten, we will eat.

'The natives, man,' the governor was saying impatiently. 'Did you get the natives? How many? Living or destroyed?'

'No natives have been got, sir,' Rooke said. This part was easy. 'Not living. Not destroyed.'

'Well, man?' Wyatt was peering into Rooke's face as if to prise the words out of his mouth. 'Well?'

'The natives eluded us, sir,' Rooke said.

'Tch!' The governor's face creased in annoyance. 'Speak up, man, how did that come about?' he demanded. 'Speak up, Lieutenant Rooke, come, man!'

'It was a failure,' Rooke began.

Remembered the firelight, Warungin laughing. The hatchet, shiny along its blade where someone had so recently been employed to put the keenest edge he could on the iron. Silk, smiling, his eyes sliding sideways.

'Sir, it was badly done,' he said.

The words had come back to him. It was a relief like a sneeze to expel them at the governor.

'It was a wicked plan, sir, I am sorry to have been persuaded to comply with the order. I would not for any reason ever again obey a similar order.'

The governor's face was slack with astonishment. Rooke watched him, saw all his prospects wither like a leaf in the fire. It was a weightless sensation. He saw it on the governor's face, irreversible, and felt nothing but relief.

Something was finished for him.

'You are speaking out of turn, Lieutenant,' Wyatt said. 'Mind your words, sir!'

Wyatt was no friend of his but Rooke saw that he was straining, like a man holding a dam, to prevent catastrophe. He was freshly shaved, as was the governor. Rooke caught a whiff of the astringent that Barber used on them.

They were three men on a sandy track, the coarse patter of gum leaves around them agitating in the breeze, a bird nearby making a noise like a creaking door.

'Sir, your orders were a most gravely wrong thing, I regret beyond words my part in the business.'

'But was anyone killed, Lieutenant?' the governor insisted as if he had not heard. 'How many were got?'

His prim-lipped manner set Rooke alight.

'I beg your pardon, sir, but that is beside the point. The

intention of evil was there which is all that God sees when he looks into our hearts.'

He saw the governor flinch at the word *God* and was surprised at himself for using it. It sounded like a cheap trick to silence the governor, when what he truly felt was that God was just a way for a man to interrogate his own heart.

'By Jove, sir,' the governor said, 'you are mighty sure of yourself for a junior officer, and mighty free with the Almighty's name!'

There was an awkwardness about this—*mighty* and *Almighty*—that made all three men pause and listen to the words ringing together.

'I will ask, Lieutenant Rooke, that you attend me at midday at Government House.'

And then he was gone. Wyatt took long strides to catch him up, glancing back at where Rooke was already turning towards his future.

He would go to his hut on the point. He would light his fire, boil water, make tea. Sit outside with his back against the wall, where the morning sun warmed the planks.

Depending on when the ships arrived from England, he might have a few weeks or a few months to sit there. He would go on measuring the rainfall, taking the temperature of the air. He might even find one or two more stars and add a few more words to the notebooks.

But sooner or later, His Majesty's grand machine would

take him into itself. He would be sent away. He would stand and listen as a court pronounced his sentence. Then he would be taken from that place and be obliged to submit to one kind of death or another: the death of the body or the death of the future.

By the time he entered the settlement, the stars could no longer be seen, the sky arching over him now a limpid early-morning blue. But they were still there, hanging in their appointed places. The earth would turn forever and sunset would follow sunrise into eternity, and the glory of the stars would blaze out whether or not anyone saw them.

PART FIVE

Antigua, 1836

A lmost fifty years later the earth still turned and the stars
still burned, and Daniel Rooke still looked up and
watched them.

He had learned that the naked eye could see things a telescope could not. The exquisite instruments of astronomy could
add new stars to the sum of the world's knowledge, but it took
a soul to wonder at the beauty of those already discovered.

They had not hanged him, for which he had gone on his
knees and given thanks to God. But when they told him he
might continue in the service, on condition that he apologise to
James Gilbert and accept a loss of rank to ensign, he refused.
By then he knew why he had been spared, and it was not to
serve His Majesty. He went straight from the court to offer
himself to another cause.

That cause had taken him back to a place he had never thought to revisit: Antigua. He marvelled at the symmetry of it. In Antigua he had once watched a young lieutenant of marines hanged for disobeying. He too had disobeyed but had been spared, and it seemed only right that Antigua should take his life and make use of it.

Now that life was fading, a star at dawn. He lay awake in the dark. Sunrise was some time off, but the window was a grey square. The tropical dawn would come too quickly, that brilliant Caribbean light that an invalid longed to shut out. Waiting for darkness was what he did now, as he had done when he was an astronomer. He thought the final darkness might not be far off.

He lay still, hardly breathing. There was a short space of time in which he was blessedly conscious only of existing. He savoured it. Then the pain returned, the pounding fullness in the head, the pangs behind the eyeballs, the aching in his shoulders, his back, his legs. It was a matter of willing time to pass, so that he might either die or recover.

Beyond the window the parrots chattered in the guava tree. Another day had to be lived through in this hot and weary bed.

The curtain, broken along its rings, still dangled lopsided as it had for every day of his illness, a shred of lining hanging down. He knew the curtain, the broken rings, that tongue of fabric, to the point of weariness. Day after day lying on the bed, he had stitched up the rip, reattached the rings, made it neat and orderly. But only in his mind's eye. It was weeks since he had had the strength to do anything more strenuous than sit up in bed, move to the commode, creep back again between the sheets.

Now he could make out his other familiars, the constellations of mildew on the ceiling and the cracks in the floor tile that made the shape of France. In his busy mind he had a pail of hot soapy water, a scrubbing brush. The cracks were full of dirt, the tiles themselves clouded across their terracotta surfaces. It was interesting to observe—or had been, the first hundred times—how the pattern of dirt revealed, in a way otherwise invisible, the slight unevennesses in the laying of the tiles. Where one corner was lower than its neighbour by a fraction, the dirt had settled, undisturbed. Where an edge rode high the passage of feet had worn it clean. If for any reason you needed to create an absolutely flat surface—for some experiment involving metal balls and their movement, for example—this would be a way to make sure of it. If he should ever find himself needing such a perfect surface, he would remember how you could use dirt.

He took it as a good sign, that he could still have such orderly and deductive thoughts.

The servant-woman, Henrietta, was good. But she had enough on her hands looking after him. Even before he fell ill, she stayed only out of a sense of honour. He had not been able to pay her for perhaps a year.

'You have been good for us,' she always said when he apologised. 'For me, and for us.'

She meant, of course, the slaves. He had given his life for them.

Well, that was a little melodramatic. He was not yet thirty when he had begun to give his life for them. He was seventy-four now, lying on this hot bed. Call it two-thirds, roughly, something like two-thirds of a life.

Actually, it was twenty-two thirty-sevenths of a life. He wondered how sick he would have to be for numbers to leave him, that craving for the exact.

Two-thirds of a life, then, let us say, that had begun with such promise. Then he had made his choice, and it had brought him here: to this house on the hill above English Harbour.

All those who had exclaimed at his prospects had fallen away long ago and all those he had loved—wife, son and daughter—were dead or elsewhere now. If a man lived as long as he had, he supposed things could not be otherwise. Now it was just himself and Henrietta.

He could hear her clanking downstairs in the kitchen, and the mewing of the cat wanting its breakfast.

Henrietta would bring him a slice of mango from the tree outside, a plate of cold boiled yam from last night. He wanted neither, but she would bring them and scold him, in her quiet way, hold up the mango until he took a bite, wipe his chin for him when the juice ran down.

A bowl of oatmeal would be good. He had loved oatmeal as a child. Portsmouth, forever shiny in the rain, and his mother's oatmeal, warm and sweet, fat with cream. In Antigua oatmeal was unknown. He supposed it could be bought from the ships that carried other luxuries from England, but only if you had money.

He had bought Henrietta at auction, when he still had money. By then he was used to it, standing with the other men and counting upwards aloud, turn and turn about with them, until they stopped. How many had he bought? He had started a list in the beginning, but left off after a time. For once, the number did not matter. He could only say, *I bought as many as I could.*

Bought and freed, of course, and how they hated him for that, the men around him in the auction yard. They had agreed among themselves, and bid the price up and up to ruin him faster.

Now there was nothing, just the water in the well, the mangoes on the trees, the yams in the garden.

'Go,' he had said, trying to be stern, when the last of the money was gone. 'I cannot pay you, you must find another place.' She had not tried to argue, only shaken her head and pressed her lips together like a child refusing medicine.

He supposed he should be sorry for it now, that choice he had made forty-six years ago. He tried out the idea in his mind. *Regret. Remorse.* He tested the words against what he felt. His head ached, his body pained him in every joint, the light hurt his eyes. He wished his wife were still alive. He would like to see his sister Anne one more time, and taste oatmeal once more, and feel the soft Portsmouth rain on his face.

All these things he felt. But he did not seem to be feeling regret. The words of regret could be summoned, but not the pang.

Regret, glimpsed out of the corner of the eye, flickered, flamed, expired.

He heard Henrietta greeting someone downstairs, the rumble of a man's voice, and could imagine it: Henrietta, a freshly washed once-red bandana bound around her black hair, and Redoubt the postman.

Through the open window he heard sounds of sweeping, and then the regular thump as a rug was beaten. Someone sang a snatch of melody, called out, there was a prolonged splash as water cascaded from something into something else. A rooster crowed triumphantly. Soon Henrietta would come up, would push back the ragged curtain and turn to look at him.

Indeed, here was her footfall on the stairs. The matting had gone long ago, so he could hear every step of her bare feet, quiet though they were. Here she was, and in her hand the old white dish with, yes, the slice of mango and there it was too, the wedge of greyish yam.

He would eat a mouthful, just to bring a smile to her face. There was a mock-hurt she did that he could not bear to see.

He knew it was only pretence, as you might pretend for a child, but still he would yield to it. He would eat the yam first, that delicate earthen taste, then the mango, sweet, fragrant, its texture almost meaty.

'Slow, Mr Rooke,' Henrietta whispered. 'Slow now and easy.'

When he had eaten a mouthful of each, he lay back. The mango was sweet to the tongue but it left an aftertaste with a bitter element. He wanted to wash it away with a sip of water but could not find the energy to sit up and drink.

The room was growing hot. He could feel the sweat, a cool drop sliding down his cheek. There was the tiresomely familiar curtain, the cracked tile, the mildew. He thought he could not bear to live through another day of the light crawling around the room, waiting for nightfall.

He heard himself sigh out all his air in a sound that was half groan, half wail. Henrietta leaned forward and she sat for a long time holding his fingers in hers, caressing them. He could feel the skin of her fingers, slippery, smooth, warm against his own.

Putuwa. That was the word Tagaran had taught him. *Putuwa*, and he had written the meaning into his little book: *to warm one's hand by the fire and then to squeeze gently the fingers of another person.*

There, on the far side of the world, it would be dusk. Tagaran, if still alive, would be a grown woman with grown children. She might have grandchildren, skinny and laughing like the child she had been when she had made a friend of Daniel Rooke.

She would remember him. Of that he was certain. She would tell her children about him, the *Berewalgal* who had been her friend when she was a girl. Who had had such difficulty with her name, she had to say it ten times! Who wrote it all down in two blue notebooks, so that the words would be fixed there forever.

Did she wonder what had become of the notebooks, the record of their conversations, written down for anyone who ever opened them and read? She would know, he thought, that he would keep them always.

The books had travelled with him to London on *Gorgon*, and then to Africa, all those years, and they were with him still, in the top drawer of the dresser in the corner. But he had never got them out, never read them. It was enough for him to know they were there. When he and Tagaran were both dead, when their children's children were dead, the notebooks would tell the story of a friendship like no other.

He had hoped to go back. He had always hoped that. Here on these islands, with black faces all around, he had seemed closer to her. Had felt himself to be travelling towards her, only a slip of land and a single ocean between him and New South Wales. He knew now, with the clarity of fever, that he would never go back there. New South Wales was as unreachable as any other past.

He did not need to look at the notebooks to remember every detail of New South Wales. He knew how it was there in the twilight. The land lost its light before the sky. The water gathered up the last of the radiance and held it, gleaming and shifting.

If he were to go back to that night on the sand of Botany Bay, would he make the same choice again, knowing that this was where it would lead him: to the raucous birds in the guava tree outside, the voices drifting up to the window, this hot room with the circling flies, the man on the bed looking at the pattern of mildew on the ceiling like dark stars?

✳

On his last morning in New South Wales he had woken before dawn. Through the open door he could see a few stars, although the sky was beginning to lighten around them.

Down in Sydney Cove, *Gorgon* waited to take him to England. It was bad luck that the long-awaited ships had finally arrived so soon after his interview with the governor. *You know I do not have the power to convene a court-martial*, His Excellency had said. His voice had trembled with anger. *But you will be sent back at the earliest opportunity, Lieutenant, to face the consequences of your actions.*

He had once thought to spend the rest of his life in New South Wales, but *the earliest opportunity* had turned out to be no more than a month.

There was a good breeze, he could hear the harbour slapping itself up against the rocks at the foot of the point. As soon as it was dawn they would ready *Gorgon* to sail. There would be no timekeeper to be wound on this voyage, and no new land at the end of it, only the unknown years of the rest of his life.

He got up and went outside. There was Betelgeuse and, along with it, as it had always been, the white blaze of Rigel.

They had been there since the beginning. Whatever the beginning was. Would be still there when the speck of matter called Daniel Rooke was no longer even a name on a forgotten gravestone, when the gravestone itself had worn away, grain by grain. Even then, Rigel and Betelgeuse would still be travelling together across the sky.

He had lit his fire, made himself a last dish of sweet-tea. *Warraburra*. Took his chair outside and sat there with his back to the wall as he had so often before, watching the sun rise one last time. He found himself taking large breaths like sighs and there was a coldness about his heart. A gilded bird, one of the white parrots caught by the sun's first rays, flapped magnificently across the patch of blue sky between the treetops.

*

At noon *Gorgon* cast off from its mooring and the blocks rattled and squealed as the sails were raised. He stood at the stern and looked towards the point the natives knew as Tarra, and which he had tried to name after Dr Vickery, but which people seemed determined to call after himself.

He could see the roof of his hut, and the brave little teepee of the observatory. On the very tip of the point, on the rocks below the hut, he could see a few natives. Among them he could just make out the figure of Tagaran.

She had arrived that morning, not leaping down the rocks as she usually did. They had barely spoken. There was nothing to say. But while he buckled up his bag, and clipped the latches on the sea-chest, and sat on it waiting for the men to come and carry it to the ship, she crouched over his little fire. She held her hands out to it—so close he thought she must have burned her palms—and then came over and sat beside him on the chest.

As she had done on another occasion, she took his hands between hers. He felt her fingers pressing and smoothing, transferring their heat to his. He closed his eyes. His skin had taken on the warmth of hers so he no longer knew which was hers and which his.

When the men came for his sea-chest Rooke and Tagaran looked at each other, looked away. He followed the men up the rocks, along the ridge. At the top he did not turn. He kept his hand closed tight around itself, around the warmth she had put there, and went on, down the hill, along the track to where the boats were waiting.

But now, leaning on the stern rail as the ship gathered way, he could see her down on the very end of the point. She was standing on the rock from which he had once watched a man spear a fish and tuck it into his belt cord. She was so far out that the waves were washing over her feet at each respiration of the water. He found himself smiling: she was as close to *Gorgon* as she could get while remaining on land.

As the wind filled the sails and *Gorgon* picked up speed down the harbour, he waved, and she answered straight away, her arm drawing one large shape through the air. Between them across the water a long thread stretched out, spinning out longer and longer as their figures grew small.

Soon Tagaran become indistinguishable from the rocks around her, the rocks indistinguishable from the headland, the headland nothing more than a distant part of the landscape. Tagaran was invisible now, but she was a part of everything he could see, like the faintest, most distant star, sending its steady light out towards him across space.

Author's note

This is a work of fiction, but it was inspired by recorded events.

Briefly, they are these: on board the First Fleet that brought convicts to Australia in 1788 was a young lieutenant of marines, William Dawes. Although nominally a soldier, he was a considerable scholar in astronomy, mathematics and languages. The record he left of the language of the indigenous people of the Sydney area is by far the most extensive we have. It contains not only word lists and speculations about the grammatical structure of the language, but conversations between him and the indigenous people, particularly a young girl, Patyegarang. Between the lines of these exchanges is what seems to be a relationship of mutual respect and affection.

In December 1790, one of the governor's gamekeepers was

mortally wounded by a spear. Dawes was one of a party of soldiers sent out to punish the tribe from which the attacker was said to come. Their orders were to capture six indigenous men and bring them back to the settlement, but if that were not possible they were to kill six, cut off their heads, and bring them back in bags provided for the purpose.

Dawes at first refused to take part, but was persuaded. On his return he announced that he regretted his decision, and if ordered to do anything similar again he would refuse. The governor would have court-martialled him for insubordination if the mechanism for court-martial had been available to him.

Earlier, Dawes had expressed a desire to settle in New South Wales, but was sent back to Britain when his tour of duty ended. He never returned to Australia, but worked for the rest of his life in the movement for the abolition of slavery, in London, Africa and the West Indies. He spent his last years in Antigua where, after Abolition, he established schools for former slaves. He died there in 1836.

*

I made extensive use of historical sources in this novel, and in particular Dawes' language notebooks. All the Cadigal words and conversations in this book are quoted verbatim from those notebooks with the kind permission of the School of Oriental and African Studies, London, (reference MS 41645) and after